A SECOND CHANCE FOR

CARYS

WELSH REBELS

VIRGINIE MARCONATO

OLIVER-HEBER BOOKS

Prologue

J ames Mortimer had never believed in miracles.

The succession of tragic events in his life had made it very hard for him to believe in a benevolent god watching over mortals with the tender care of a father. He was more inclined to think the god in question cruel and intent on spreading misery for his twisted amusement. Why else would he have taken the people he'd loved from him, and left him to deal with the awful pain alone? No, miracles didn't exist, he'd known it for years. But today, he was forced to see that the god could, on occasion, at least show some compassion.

Brow arched, he reread the letter in his hand.

I will be home at the end of the month with my bride, Branwen ferch Gethin, her sister, Eirwen, and her mother, Carys. My father, Richard, will also be with us. From now on, he will live at Sheridan Manor. Please get everything ready for us.

Well, James thought ruefully, if that wasn't a miracle, he

didn't know what was. Or rather, *two* miracles. Not only had Matthew Hunter been reunited with his long-lost father, a man he had hated all his life for abandoning his mother—or so he'd thought—but he was now married. To a Welsh woman no less. Not a man easily given to mirth, James afforded a chuckle. This, he would have to see for himself.

How had the woman managed to ensnare him in so little time? He had made no secret of his animosity toward the Welsh when he'd been forced to leave England a little over a year ago to follow his brother. When Connor had agreed to marry a Welsh woman on the king's orders, Matthew had urged him to refuse.

It seemed that, unlike what he'd feared at first, the Welsh weren't all savages. At least, the women weren't. So much so that he'd married one of them when James had started to wonder if the man he'd long considered as a son would ever settle down.

Tucking the missive into his tunic, he gave his orders to the servants. Matthew's bedchamber was to be given a good airing, the rushes replaced throughout the castle, the tapestries dusted. The bride's mother and sister would share a bedchamber in the east wing, which was the most comfortable, and Richard would be allocated a room in the west wing. It would be good to have people at Sheridan Manor again, it had been rather lonely since the two brothers' departure.

A few days later, everything was ready. Just as he was thanking the servants for their hard work, a rider cantered through the gate, heralding the imminent arrival of the travelers. Later that day, a small retinue was spotted on the road from Wales. Perfect timing.

James walked over to the gate to welcome everyone.

Chapter One

England, May 1297

E ngland.

So this was it. Carys looked at the landscape surrounding her, finding it not so different from the rolling hills she was used to. And yet. Yet it could not be more different. She was now in enemy country, away from home, away from everything and everyone she knew, with little hope of ever returning. The Welsh part of her life was over.

Of course, she could have stayed behind, but she had been unable to let her daughters go on their own. The two sisters, who were only her daughters by choice, would now reside in England. Branwen, the eldest, had just married a powerful English lord's brother and he had agreed Eirwen could come live with them at Sheridan Manor. When given the option of going as well, Carys had taken it. How could she not? They were her only family. She would not be separated from them.

But *England...*

Carys had been twenty-six years old when the English king, Edward, had invaded her country. Since then, she had heard the English described as the enemy, and it was true she had seen some horrible deeds since they had implanted themselves in the conquered land. But she refused to believe they were all the same. Matthew Hunter, her new son-in-law, at least, was a good man, as was his brother, Connor, who everyone agreed was the fairest and most efficient ruler Castell Esgyrn had ever seen. They were heading for the two men's family seat so she had hopes she would be made welcome there, and not be treated as an oddity, or a savage. There was little chance Matthew, who loved Branwen fiercely, would allow anyone to bother his wife or her kin.

Still, on her first night on English soil, she barely slept for nervousness. Then, little by little, as she realized that nothing she was seeing could be called worrying or even out of the ordinary, she started to relax. Perhaps this would be all right.

By the time they came into view of Sheridan Manor, five days later, she had lost most of her diffidence. But the first glimpse of her future residence stole her breath away.

Arglwydd Mawr!

It was even grander than she had supposed. How had Branwen married a man who was, despite his lack of title, master of such a place? She stole a glance at her daughter. Atop a magnificent bay palfrey with her husband by her side, himself riding a snow-white stallion, she had never looked more regal or, which was the important thing, happier. Carys could never thank Matthew enough for having given Branwen the life she deserved. If that life was to be in England, then so be it.

As long as her daughters were happy, she could face anything. As a woman well past her fortieth year, and a widow, her life was over anyway.

Later that afternoon, the retinue passed through the gate and came to a halt. Half a dozen men were waiting in the bailey to welcome them. A rider had been sent ahead, so they would have been warned about their master's arrival. A tall, elegant man dressed in black approached. The steward, probably. She'd heard about this James Mortimer who had made it possible for Matthew to be reunited with his father Richard, a humble carpenter. By all accounts the man was efficiency personified. Judging from his stern demeanor, she could well believe it.

Matthew jumped down from his horse and addressed him with a smile. Carys did not even try to understand what they told each other. She only knew a handful of English words, and she doubted the two men were thanking one another or counting up to ten She would have to learn the language, she reminded herself for the hundredth time, now that she had arrived in her new home. Her life would be hell otherwise.

The man glanced at her and she couldn't help inhaling in surprise. He had the blackest eyes she had ever seen. The *only* black eyes she had ever seen, she amended quickly. She hadn't even known eyes could be black up until now. The effect was stunning, rather like staring into the night sky with all the stars sucked out of it, leaving only the dizzying void. But considering his complexion, any other eye color would have jarred, rather like seeing a stray crystal amongst a sea of obsidian. Everything about him was sombre. His hair was the blueish hue of a raven's wing, even if it was streaked with silver stands at the temples, his skin was darker than the average person's and he was dressed fully in black.

All in all, he was the very image of the English warrior she had dreaded to meet. Not that his expression was in any way threatening or that he was carrying any weapons. He didn't have any scabbard and he looked mild-mannered and kind. But striking nonetheless.

While he turned his attention back to Matthew, she jumped down from the saddle with undisguised relief. A week on the road had taken its toll on her body. Even as a young woman, she would have found the trip taxing, as she had not ridden horses often. There simply had been no need.

"All right, Mam?" Branwen asked, guessing she would be stiff after the long ride.

"Aye, *cariad*, don't worry about me." Carys nodded toward the people assembled in front of them. "The English will want to welcome their new mistress, go speak to them."

After one last smile, Branwen turned her attention back to the men.

"I think you and your guests will find everything to your satisfaction," James told his master, noting that the young man had never looked better. Marriage seemed to suit him.

"I'm sure I will. When have you let anyone down, James?"

"Never, I hope."

James acknowledged the praise with a slight bow. Matthew was the only one here to call him by his Christian name, instead of "Mortimer." But then again, he was not of noble blood either, only Lord Sheridan's milk brother. Secretly, James had always considered him like the son he'd never seen grow up. By coincidence, his little Edward had died only weeks after Matthew's mother, Rose. The bastard son of the poor maid had been raised by the late Lord Sheridan alongside his heir, Connor. But James had been the one to teach him all he knew. The orphan and the father without a son had been natural allies, and helped one another.

Putting those unhelpful considerations to one side, he turned his attention to the rest of the retinue. The two women standing either side of Matthew looked rather similar to one another, with their long, dark hair and full, red lips, and both appeared as if they could be his bride. Which one was Branwen, he wondered? The third woman, slightly to the left of the group, was blonde and markedly older. He barely spared her a glance. Probably a lady's maid they had brought from Esgyrn Castle to assist the two women. Behind her was Richard, Matthew's long lost father, who nodded his greetings. The rest of the group consisted of the men at arms who would have ensured the safety of the women during the travel, and a huge gray wolfhound.

"Meet my wife, Branwen." Matthew wrapped an arm around the waist of the woman to his right, who could not help a blush. She had extraordinary golden eyes, James noticed, of a color rarely seen.

"You are right welcome at Sheridan Manor, my lady."

No one pointed out that, strictly speaking, she had no right to the title, being married to a man of low birth. Everyone here called Matthew "my lord," anyway.

"Thank you. I am glad to be here."

"This is her sister, Eirwen." The other dark-haired girl gave a brief nod. James returned it, noting that her eyes were of a more common brown. "And this is Carys, their mother."

Ah, he'd gotten it completely wrong. The older woman was not a servant at all. Of course! He'd been told the Welsh bride would bring her mother with her, so he should have guessed who she was, as there were no other women in the retinue. In his defense, with her fair hair and blue eyes, she looked completely different from her daughters, so much so that he had not for a moment thought she could be Matthew's mother-in-law. And... perhaps to be more soon. The way Richard was hovering by the woman's side indicated a desire to further their acquaintance. Or perhaps they were already involved with each other. It was possible. They were of an age, and they had spent a month in Wales together, as well as a week on the road. It would not surprise him if the carpenter had been struck and tried to woo the woman.

Because now that James had taken the time to look at her, he saw that she was, well, striking.

Some women looked good in their young years, before losing some of their appeal when life made their features harden. Others only became more attractive with age. He suspected that Carys was one of them. Not that she would not have looked good twenty years ago, he imagined. But maturity undoubtedly suited her.

The lines following the corner of her eyes and bracketing her mouth were testimony to a life rich in happiness and laughter. Her eyes were of the celestial blue he'd always associated with innocence and honesty. Her mouth was rosy pink, her skin creamy white, her hair bursting with shades ranging from copper to silver to gold, her dress the kind of green only ever seen in spring, on newly grown grass. She was vibrant with energy and colors. Next to this explosion of life he felt rather drab, like a dried leaf would be, while lying on the ground next to a tree in full bloom.

If that was what Welsh women looked like, then it was no wonder both Connor and Matthew had fallen in love with them.

Carys blushed slightly under his scrutiny, as if ill at ease. How would she feel here, in a foreign country, away from everything and everyone she knew? Not only that, but as a Welsh woman, she would be under the impression she'd entered the wolves' lair.

He frowned. Why was he worrying about all that? He should be ushering Matthew and his new wife into the great hall, offering them refreshments, seeing to the comfort of everyone and giving the grooms their orders, not staring at a woman he didn't know and wondering how she would fare in England, no matter how beautiful she looked.

"Please, let's get you all settled. You'll find everything you need in the great hall. If you will follow me?"

Unable to resist, he had addressed this last sentence to Carys. But instead of moving, she shook her head. Was she offended? Why? What had he said?

Branwen placed a hand on her mother's arm. "Mam doesn't

speak a word of English or understand more than 'yes' and 'no', I'm afraid." With this apology, she translated his words to her mother.

Carys nodded and surprised him, and probably her daughter as well, when she turned to him and said, very distinctively: "Thank you."

"Well." Branwen let out a tinkle of a laugh. "I guess she does know a few words. I had no idea."

It didn't take James long to understand why Matthew might have fallen under the woman's spell. Her beauty was not just surface deep. Her voice was sultry, her accent endearing, her manners delightful. He looked at Carys again, wondering how mother and daughter could look so different. She was as fair as Branwen was dark, her eyes, as he'd remarked before, were blue rather than golden, and her face a completely different shape. All in all, she looked nothing like her or Eirwen. Maybe the girls took after their father, then. Where was the man? Had he decided to remain in Wales? Was he dead, perhaps?

He started. Here he was again, allowing himself to get distracted by the Welsh woman when he should be ushering the hungry travelers into the great hall.

With slow deliberation, he turned away from her. "This way."

"Good boy. I bet you are itching to have a good run, aren't you? Don't let me stop you. I wish I could go with you."

Carys ruffled Silver's hair affectionately. The dog had been given to Branwen by Matthew some months ago and had become a family favorite. That morning she had taken him with her on her walk because, unlike the people at Sheridan Manor, he didn't mind her speaking in Welsh. It would take her a while to make friends here, since she could only communicate with her two daughters.

While she sat on a log to watch the river flow in the sunshine, as she's predicted, Silver shot away to expend his pent up energy.

When he came back a moment later, he was accompanied by another wolfhound the color of ripe wheat.

"You've found a special friend, I see," she told him with a smile.

The dog would belong to someone at Sheridan Manor and might even be a distant relative of his. Matthew's brother, Connor, had probably taken some of his hounds to Castell Esgyrn when he'd come to marry his Welsh bride.

Castell Esgyrn.

She'd always wondered why that name had been chosen. Bones Castle seemed an unlikely, gloomy name for such an elegant castle. More to the point, she was surprised to see that the thought of her old home did not provoke any pangs of nostalgia within her. But after all, as long as she was with Branwen and Eirwen, she could be anywhere. At the village, no one would miss her. She had not even minded leaving Dewi's grave behind. Her beloved husband would live forever in her heart, that was all that mattered, she didn't need a piece of stone to remember him by. When she thought of him, it was as a man vibrant with life, not as a skeleton buried underground. She heard his laugh, his declarations of love, his groans of pleasure. Would those memories fade away with time?

She fervently prayed they wouldn't, because then she would be truly alone.

A voice cut through her musings, and Silver's friend bounded in the direction of the caller, obviously his master. Carys watched as James Mortimer appeared from behind a cluster of trees. He was dressed in black, just like the day of their arrival, just like every day, in fact. Every time she'd caught a glimpse of him, he'd been the same stark, slightly forbidding figure. She had made sure not to find herself alone with him, something she didn't do with anyone else. Not only would they be unable to communicate, but she could not deny he impressed her.

Avoiding him now would be impossible, though, so she stayed where she was. Walking away when he had seen her would just appear rude. But what could they tell each other? Nothing. He spoke even less Welsh than she spoke English.

Feeling at a loss, but not wanting to stand there like a fool, she pointed at her dog. "Silver."

To her relief, James seemed to understand she was introducing him and decided to help her along in her pitiful attempt at conversation.

"Goldie," he answered, pointing at the other wolfhound in the same way she had.

A gleam appeared in his black eyes. It seemed to her that he found the association of the two names amusing. Why? She would make sure to ask Branwen later what "Goldie" meant.

"It's very beautiful here," she tried next, looking at the river flowing down below. This time it was clear James had no idea what she was talking about. He shrugged. In a moment he would walk away, bored by the awkwardness of the exchange, and she could not blame him. He probably had better things to do than talk to a stranger he could not understand.

Carys was wondering what to do when Sliver, who'd been sniffing and nuzzling at his new friend with sudden interest, mounted her with undisguised enthusiasm. There was no need for translation. This time they could both understand what was happening. Carys' cheeks started to burn.

James arched a brow and she had the feeling he was fighting a smile. She found herself wondering what *she* could do to coax such a reaction out of him. She had rarely seen a more impassive man.

All too soon, Silver let go of his new friend, who Carys now knew to be a female—and possibly pregnant. The two dogs spent a long moment nuzzling at each other. Fascinated, she watched on. There was such tenderness in the caresses that something tugged at her heart. It felt almost human. Suddenly she did miss home, and Dewi, terribly.

"I think we might have a litter of beautiful puppies soon," she could not help but say out loud.

There was no answer.

James had already left.

Chapter Two

"Forgive me. I didn't know someone would be here."

James had gone to the little room at the back of the solar to return the ledgers he'd taken earlier—and found himself face to face with Carys.

She shook her head, indicating she could not answer him, as he'd thought. She would have no idea what he'd said, even if she must have understood he was apologizing for having almost bumped into her.

He scowled, barely refraining a growl. Damn it all, this was impossible. How long would it be until she learned to speak his language? She had been at Sheridan Manor for more than two weeks already and she seemed to have no intention of making it easier for people to communicate with her. It appeared as if she was happy to take long walks in the forest and talk to no one else other than her daughters and her dog when she was in the castle.

Her dog. Silver, the wolfhound. It had been excruciating to stand there and watch as he'd mounted Goldie the other day. Though the two indiscreet lovers had been animals, it had been a disturbingly intimate scene to witness in the company of a woman he desired.

Desired. Yes.

The realization had taken him by surprise, but he desired the Welsh woman like he had not desired a woman since Joanne's death.

He'd been struck by her allure the moment he had seen her dismount from her weary horse in the bailey. In view of this unexpected reaction, he had intended to spend time with her and get to know her better, see where this unexpected attraction could lead. Unfortunately, he had not counted on the frustration it would create to not be able to have any conversation with her whatsoever. As intriguing as Carys was, at the moment, he got as much satisfaction out of her as he would out of a wooden statue of a woman. A real pity, because he suspected that the Welsh woman would be all fire, exactly what he needed to thaw the ice that had started to encase his heart. He'd seen her joyous with Branwen, mischievous with Eirwen, playful with Silver. She was full of life, unable to hide her feelings.

But with him she was quiet and discreet, and this because they could not exchange more than basic greetings. It was infuriating.

As he was wondering how to take his leave without appearing too rude, the door to the solar, which he'd left open on his way in, closed with a bang.

"Are you sure we can—"

A woman's voice. Branwen's? James couldn't be sure, as she had spoken in a barely audible whisper, as if not wishing to be overheard.

"Yes, I'm sure. What would be the point of being master of Sheridan Manor if I cannot take you wherever I want, whenever I want?" Matthew's voice was hoarse with need, confirming it was indeed Branwen in the other room. Too in love with his wife, he would never think of waylaying another woman. "Sit on me, Raven, like you did that first time. Make me come. Jesus, I'm bursting with the need of you."

James stole a glance toward Carys. Though, mercifully, she would have been unable to make sense of the words, she could not have failed to understand what was happening. It would be clear to her that the man in the next room was about to take his lover with all the passion he was capable of. This was excruciating, and the worst was yet to come. Soon they would hear grunting, moaning, panting. It would be bad enough for him, but the woman about to ride her husband senseless was Carys' own daughter. No one should have to listen to their children making love.

Had she recognized who the two lovers were?

Yes, she had, if her horrified expression was anything to go by.

He could not let her face this. It had been bad enough to watch Goldie and Silver copulate the other day, they would not today listen to Matthew and Branwen make love.

Taking her by the hand, he cleared his throat loudly to warn the couple that, contrary to what they had hoped, they weren't alone and were about to be interrupted.

"Fuck!"

There was a series of curses and the rustling of material, betraying the fact that the frenzied lovers were restoring order to their clothes. James gave them a moment to make themselves decent. When he and Carys finally entered the room, Matthew was standing in front of his wife, shielding her from view, doing what he could to minimize her embarrassment. Placed behind his big body, Branwen would be able to avoid seeing who had almost caught her in the act of making love to her husband—her own mother. It was a relief.

"Forgive us, we were just—"

"Yes, yes," Matthew snarled, not best pleased at the interruption. "Just go."

James didn't need to be told twice. Still holding Carys by the hand, he made his way to the staircase.

Once they were safely out of earshot of the two reckless lovers, he turned to face her.

"I'm sorry about that." To help convey his meaning, he raised both his palms in an apologetic gesture. Though it was not his fault, he could not help but say something. He'd left without a word the other day in the forest, and had regretted it ever since. It was not her fault that learning a new language was not something that could be accomplished in two days.

Carys bit her lip. "Branwen?" she asked, pointing in the direction of the solar.

James hesitated. This was awkward. He had not expected her to ask confirmation about the identity of the lovers. Then he saw the anguish in her eyes. Because she hadn't understood what Matthew had said, and she hadn't seen the woman hidden behind his bulk, she was worried her daughter's husband had been sneaking around with a mistress under his wife's nose. An understandable concern. Too many men he knew would do just that. As embarrassing as it was, he could not let her worry on this score. It was not fair to anyone. The couple in the solar hadn't been doing anything wrong, and Matthew did not deserve to have his morals put into doubt just because he couldn't keep his hands off his wife.

Being in love and reckless was a feeling James remembered too well.

"Yes. It was Branwen." For good measure, he nodded. For once, he was grateful he and Carys weren't able to communicate better, as he didn't want to talk to her about the fact that she had almost overheard her daughter riding her husband.

He could tell his answer had reassured her but she didn't

know what to say. For a long, uncomfortable moment, they stared at one another. What was the point of staying here, he wondered? He should just leave.

After one last bow, he did just that.

How embarrassing.

Carys would never have admitted to anyone, including herself, that the urgency in Matthew's voice, the very explicit noises she had heard, the realization of what was happening in the other room, had inflamed her imagination and heated her blood. Standing next to James in that little room, she had felt her body respond in a most unsettling way. Perhaps it was due to the long abstinence imposed on her, or perhaps to the proximity of a man exuding virility, she didn't know. Either way, it was worrying.

"Holy Mother of God, have mercy on me," she said to herself.

Why did she have to feel attracted to a man like him, so stern and unyielding? Richard, who could not communicate with her any better, always went out of his way to make their encounters less awkward, using noises and hand gestures to make his meaning clear.

Not James Mortimer. He just stood there, assessing her with those unfathomable black eyes. It was as if he thought she was not worth making the effort of trying to communicate. Or was it even worse than that? Had he guessed she was not immune to his charm? Was it his way of discouraging her? Right now, in the little room, had he been as affected as she when they'd over-heard the two lovers? He had acted with decision, taking her away before it was too late, and she was grateful for it, but... but perhaps she wouldn't have minded if he had pressed her against the wall and started to—

Carys shook her head. What was happening to her? She had yet to exchange a single sentence with the man and she could not decipher his moods. The stern steward should be the last man she entertained such notions about.

Was that what the appeal was then? Was she attracted to him because she thought he could give her what she was after, a romp between the sheets with no consequences? No real connection, apart from physical pleasure? At her age, that was all she was looking for, and perhaps James Mortimer could provide it.

She had been deeply in love with her first husband, and in the eighteen years since his death, had never even considered she could fall for another man. A meaningless tryst, she could imagine. After all, she was a still a woman with needs, for all that she was a widow and she had, on occasion, given in to men's advances.

But the only problem was, a tryst with James *would* have consequences. He lived here, and so did she now. There would be no avoiding him after the deed was done.

Besides, how did you bed someone you could not talk to? Part of the pleasure was in the sharing of the moment and the exchanging of heated declarations. It would be impossible to tell James to go slower, to take her harder, to make him understand how she wanted to be touched. And did she really want someone like him in her bed? He might look good, but if he could not even smile when he was amused, would he be able or willing to let his passion burst through while making love to a woman? She would spend her time wondering if he was enjoying himself or what she was doing wrong.

In any case, there was little point asking herself those questions. There was no reason to think she would ever end up in his arms.

Resolving to push the incident, and the dour James Mortimer, out of her mind, Carys headed off toward the forest, taking Silver with her. With Branwen's help, Avice, the cook, had asked if she could go gather some herbs for tonight's meal. Carys had been only too happy to agree. Busy filling her basket with nettles, wild garlic and dandelion leaves, she managed to forget all about the steward.

But that night in bed, her mind started to meander down dangerous paths.

Where did James sleep? Did he sleep naked? Was he big and dark all over? Her cheeks burst into flames when the question crossed her mind. Had she just tried to imagine the color of his intimate hairs and the size of his manhood? Yes, yes she had, and this while lying next to her young daughter. By her side, Eirwen, was breathing evenly, lost to the innocence of sleep.

Horrified at her wantonness, Carys left the bed and started to pace around the room. After a while she grew even more restless and she decided to leave. A walk over the battlements would be the very thing to clear her mind of inappropriate thinking before attempting to go to sleep. Though it was not cold, as she was only wearing her nightshift, she wrapped herself in her cloak for modesty and exited the room.

It was pitch black in the staircase and she regretted not taking a candle with her. Should she go back and light one? No, she could not risk awakening Eirwen. It took time, but feeling her way along the cold stone, she made it safely to the bottom of the stairs. Outside, the moon was casting enough light for her to get her bearings and she decided against taking a torch. Much better to have a free hand to hold the hem of her shift and cloak while she climbed the ladder to the north battlements.

She could have stayed in the bailey, of course, but she needed to feel the wind in her hair.

From the top, Carys could see miles into the distance. A silver ribbon gleamed beyond the dark forest, catching her eye. Was it the sea? She had never noticed any blue expanse of water during the day, where it would have melted into the horizon, but perhaps it truly was there? Her heart leapt. How she longed to go to the sea! Dewi had said he would take her one day, but in the end they had never made the effort to get there. Of course she could have gone on her own after his death, but somehow, it would have felt like a betrayal.

"I miss you," she murmured, sending her message to the wind. "Perhaps we will go to the sea together one day, my love."

Just then footsteps were heard and soon, someone was ascending the ladder she had climbed only moments ago. Everything within Carys dissolved. The tall, looming shape dressed in black could only belong to one man. The only other man who could have matched him for bulk at Sheridan Manor would never leave Branwen's bed in favor of wandering around at night alone.

No, this was not Matthew but James, the man she had tried to imagine naked only moments ago. She could not see him now, not when she knew she would take advantage of the darkness to stare at parts of his body she should not even consider looking at.

She stayed where she was, hidden in the shadow of a tower, still as a statue. Would he see her? And what would he do if he did? She would be unable to explain what she was doing here in English. Not that it was any of his concern. Or perhaps it was, in a manner of speaking, considering why she had left her bed in the first place.

I came out because I was getting agitated imagining how you looked naked. There. Are you satisfied? And now that you're here, could you put an end to my wondering by removing your clothes so I can see you? The moonlight might be sufficient for me to answer the most pressing question, namely—

He spoke, his voice gruff. Unsurprisingly, Carys didn't understand what he'd said but she guessed he was asking if anyone was out there. As steward, he was in charge of the safety of the place. Was he worried there was an ill-intentioned stranger about? Perhaps he had heard her talk to Dewi, perhaps he'd seen her cloak fluttering in the wind. Who knew?

She didn't move, barely dared to breathe. As if to help her vanish into the night, the moon chose that moment to hide behind a cloud, taking with it what little light had been illuminating the battlements. In her dark cloak Carys would blend in with the stone wall. The only way James would see her now was if he came within touching distance of her.

After a while, she heard his footsteps in the bailey and then saw his dark shape retreat to the main hall.

She waited a moment to make sure he was not coming back out and then descended the ladder herself. It was time to go back to bed and try to sleep.

"How pathetic," she muttered to herself as she crossed the deserted bailey. She had always spoken what was on her mind out loud. Dewi had found the habit endearing, but she knew most people were annoyed by it. Still, she could not help herself. "I came here to avoid imagining James naked and who should I see but the man hims—"

Carys fell and landed on something both softer than the stone she expected and yet too hard to be comfortable. A person. A man.

James Mortimer.

"What the—"

James stopped the curse already on his lips when he realized that the person who'd just landed on top of him was a woman. Then he saw he could swear all he wanted, as the woman in question wouldn't understand a word he'd say anyway.

Carys.

She had been the one lurking about earlier.

As he'd exited the main hall, he'd caught sight of something that could have been a fluttering cloak on the battlements. Always on the look out for trouble, he'd instantly been on his guard. Had someone scaled the ramparts? Was Sheridan Manor about to be attacked?

After straining his eyes in vain for a while, he had decided he had been mistaken and retreated back inside the hall. It was time to go to bed. He had crouched down to retrieve a key he'd dropped and the next thing he knew, a soft, warm, sweet-smelling woman had toppled over him. Yes. A woman. So warm after the chilly breeze wafting in from the sea, so soft in contrast to the stone digging in the muscles of his back, so sweet-smelling, like freshly picked herbs and something else, something, quite stupidly, he thought might be Welsh air.

Carys.

Without knowing why, he just knew it was her.

Thankfully, he had somehow managed to cushion her fall and avoid her smashing her skull on the hard floor.

The only problem was, having a soft, warm, sweet-smelling woman lying on top of him was creating havoc in the lower part of his body. Had he been thirty years younger, he might well be hard now. As he was not an excitable youth any longer, he managed to hold on to enough sanity to stop his body from responding.

"What are you doing here at this hour?" he growled, not best pleased by this development. He knew she could not understand him, much less answer, but he had to say something to defuse the tension between them.

A sentence in husky Welsh was all he got in return for his trouble. He closed his eyes and let it wash over him. He'd heard it said many times that Welsh people were barbarians and their language offensive to the ear of civilized Englishmen, but he could not agree. All he could think was that he wished he could pluck those raspy words out of Carys' mouth with a kiss.

When she fell silent he forced himself to move. There was nothing to be gained by lying there on the cold stone. Twisting his body, he scrambled back to his knees and brought himself to a standing position. All the while, he kept Carys close. Close as only two people who were about to kiss could be.

"Good night, then. Sleep well."

She never answered. For a delicious, heady moment, he thought she would raise herself onto her tiptoes and kiss him. He stilled, not wanting to discourage her. He would not take the first step, of course, but if she initiated it, he would respond. It would be one way of communicating how he felt about her, he supposed. Yes. But then what?

He waited, not knowing whether she would dare kiss him, not quite sure he wanted her to. She raised her head and whispered something. Why did it sound so enticing not to understand what she was saying? Because he could imagine what he wanted, that was why. For all he knew she had told him she wanted him to make love to her out there in the moonlight.

"Do you want me, Carys? Is that why you are staying in my arms longer than you should?"

A gasp. She wouldn't have understood the question, but she could not have failed to note that he'd called her by her name. Before he could say anything else, she turned and fled. James found himself only grasping at thin air.

English air that didn't smell of anything.

"Is there a problem?" Matthew entered the room as James was folding the piece of parchment and did not miss the frown on his face. "Can I help?"

"No, I thank you. And there isn't a problem, exactly."

James tapped his finger on the missive he'd received earlier that morning and fell deep in thought.

After his encounter with Carys, he'd spent an agitated night reliving the moment she had been draped all over him like a comforting, living blanket. By dawn he had decided he would make some effort to reach out to her. Why should she be the only one trying to be understood? Branwen could help at first, teaching him a few words of Welsh and anyway, living here now as she did, Carys was bound to pick up words of English. With time, the two of them might get to find some way of communicating.

But time was precisely what he wouldn't have, because he was about to leave.

"My sister-in-law Margaret has written to say that her youngest son and only daughter died of a mysterious illness last month," he explained to Matthew, who was still waiting for an answer. "Her only remaining son recently left to get married and has his own family to look after. She's been a widow for quite some time and is now alone in the world. I feel I should go see her."

Matthew placed a hand over his shoulder and nodded. "Of course you should. Offer the woman whatever solace you can at this difficult time."

This answer didn't surprise James. Matthew Hunter had always been a good man and a generous master. He'd guessed he would allow him to go. The only problem was, he didn't really want to. Not only had he never warmed to Margaret, but he had received the letter the very day he'd decided to do something about the attraction he felt for Carys. It felt particularly harsh.

Nevertheless, he could not voice his concerns and would have to pretend he didn't mind doing the right thing by his sister-in-law.

"Thank you. I promise to be back as soon as I can. Although I might also take this opportunity to go see my parents while I'm there."

If he had to leave Sheridan Manor anyway, he might as well make the most of it. From Margaret's village, it would only be another day's travel to his parents' hut. He hadn't visited them in years and, considering how old they were, this might be the last time he ever saw them. Though they weren't particularly close, he was their son.

Or... At least he was his mother's son, which was almost the same.

The irony of a man his age still being in a position to go see his parents was not lost on him. The couple had both entered their ninth decade, an almost unnatural age, whereas none of his four children had survived infancy. His two sons had died before reaching the age of two and his two daughters had never even drawn a single breath. It was only because he'd had to be there for Joanne that James had not gone mad with grief.

It was a cruel twist of fate. A man his age should have had to bury his parents, not his offspring.

"Do what you must, and fret not," Matthew concluded. "We will survive without you. Come back when you're ready."

"Thank you. I will."

The next morning, James left without having found the chance to have a word with Carys. But with them being unable to communicate, what would he have said anyway?

Chapter Three

Four months later

"What's the matter, Branwen *bach*?"

Carys sat down next to her daughter, who was warming her hands on the brazier in front of her. It wasn't the first time Branwen had looked preoccupied. As the summer heat had begun to fade, so had she started to get more and more withdrawn. Her daughter was not prone to such seasonal melancholy, and as she was now married to a man she loved and who worshipped her in turn, Carys couldn't help but worry. What was ailing her? Was she homesick? It was possible.

To her surprise, she herself did not feel out of place at Sheridan Manor. After her initial doubts about living in England, she had accustomed herself very well to her new surroundings. Many Welsh people felt hatred toward the English invaders, and she could understand the feeling to a certain extent. Some of them *had* abused their power. But, in truth, being here was just like being at home. Once you got to know them, you saw that the people here were just like the people she'd known all her life. Some, like Matthew and Connor, were good men and loving husbands, others like Avice and Richard were trustworthy friends. Some like the groom, the master of hounds and the washerwoman were conceited, dull as rain and with a penchant for gossip just like the baker, the miller and the brewer's wife had been in her village. There was the odd aggressive one, but really how was that any different from, say Morgan or Dafydd, who'd been all too ready to use their fists?

Mostly, they were just like her old friends and acquaintances had been, and now that she could at last communicate with them, she fit right in.

The similarities between the two peoples made the conflict between their two countries all the more ridiculous. Carys saw in ways she had not seen before how it was all just about the greed of one man, the King of England. Most likely, his subjects would have been happy left to their own devices.

"Do you want to tell me what is troubling you?"

Branwen examined her nails in an attempt at avoiding having to give an answer, but Carys knew her daughter had always welcomed the opportunity to share her burden when asked. When she finally looked at her, her eyes were filled with tears.

"I've started to bleed. Again." Unsure what to say, Carys waited. "Ah, Mam, Matthew and I have been married for months, more than half a year already and my womb has yet to quicken. I thought it would have happened by now, that I would get to hold my child in my arms in the new year, but nothing is happening. What if we can't have children?" She shook her head. "It's not as if we weren't trying either."

"No."

This, Carys knew all too well. There was no mistaking the looks her daughter and her husband exchanged whenever they thought no one was looking. And, of course, there had been the scene she and James had interrupted shortly after their arrival at

Sheridan Manor. No, Branwen and Matthew were doing all that was required to ensure a babe was conceived. That was not the problem.

Was there even a problem? She dearly hoped not.

Carys bit her bottom lip. She had always been there for Branwen but unfortunately, in this instance, she wasn't sure what to tell her. The pain of wondering if you would ever get to bear your own children, of waiting for your courses every month, their arrival betraying the fact that life had not blossomed in your womb despite all your prayers, she knew all too well. How had she not guessed the lack of children would be weighing on her daughter's mind? What happy bride did not want to start a family with the man she loved?

"Give it time. Your life was turned upside down when you met your husband, and much has happened since your wedding. You've left your country and you'll need to adapt to your new environment. Your body will need time to adjust to all the changes. It's been less than year, and you're still young, surely there is no cause for concern yet."

"I know, but... As you know, for years I took herbs to prevent conception," Branwen reminded her in a deathly voice. Thinking back to her difficult past was always painful. "What if the effect was permanent? What if after so long fighting to prevent a man's seed from taking root in it, my body had—"

Carys stopped her with a hand on the cheek. Unfortunately, she knew all about the reasons her daughter had been forced to protect herself from birthing children imposed on her by men who'd gone to her thinking only of their pleasure, and she had to admit that perhaps her fears were not unfounded.

But fretting about it would accomplish nothing. She had learned it the hard way. Better to seek advice from people who knew than struggle in her own.

"Thinking like this will do you no good whatsoever. I'm

certain your body is not damaged, but perhaps it needs some time to rid itself of the effect the plants had on it." Now that she thought about it, it would not be surprising if this were the case. "We can go and ask a midwife's advice tomorrow if you wish. Children will come in time, and if they don't, then you will make your peace with it, like I did. The important thing is for you to be happy. Are you happy?"

The question was unnecessary, and Branwen did not even hesitate. She straightened up, a defiant gleam in her eyes.

"Matthew is the man I never thought to find. I love him so."

"Is he worried about you not having conceived yet?" Was that what the problem was? Was her husband putting pressure on her, talking about the heir he wanted, making her miserable? Carys doubted it, and Branwen's horrified expression was enough to tell her that was not the issue.

"He's perfect. I know he wants children, but he's never addressed me with a single word of reproach. Esyllt told me she got with child the first night she spent with Connor, and here I am, still waiting." Her eyes filled with tears, and she bit her bottom lip. "I cannot help but think there is something wrong with me."

"There is nothing wrong with you." Carys drew her daughter into her arms the way she had when she'd been a child in need of comfort. "Now, no more crying. This is no one's fault and no cause for concern. We'll go and see Mistress Ivy, the village healer, tomorrow."

"Yes," Branwen said through her sobs.

"I'm sure you'll soon tell me you've missed your courses and I know everyone at Sheridan Manor will rejoice when your first babe is born."

An image of James Mortimer came to her mind. Why him rather than Richard, Matthew's father, she wondered? Indeed, technically, the carpenter would be the babe's grandfather, not him, even if she knew the steward had been a father figure for Matthew during his childhood.

Probably because she jumped on every opportunity to think of him.

He'd been gone for months, so long that she was starting to wonder if he would ever come back to Sheridan Manor. She had not dared broach the topic with anyone, not even with Branwen, who might be privy to what was going on, because what he did should be of no interest to her.

But try as she may, she could not get him out of her head.

The moment she had found herself draped on top of him was branded in her mind, which was little wonder. Only lovers found themselves in such a position. He had felt so strong underneath her... how would he feel *over* her?

No, not again! She had to stop thinking about him in such terms.

Clearing her throat, she squeezed Branwen's hands. "Be ready at dawn, we'll go pay the healer a visit."

Winter came and went, and soon enough, the snow began to melt.

It seemed to Carys that Branwen had taken heart since her meeting with Mistress Ivy. As promised, they had gone to the village the day after their discussion and the kind woman had reassured them in a matter-of-fact manner.

"My girl, the only thing that will stop a woman as healthy as you from conceiving is the lack of man's attention. No one but the Virgin Mother could create life without a man's seed. Or are you telling me your husband will not do his duty by you in bed? Is that what the problem is?"

Carys had found it hard to keep a straight face when Branwen's cheeks had gone the color of a summer sunset. "No. That is not the problem."

"I see." Mistress Ivy's eyes had twinkled in appreciation. "Then I'm sure I will soon be summoned to deliver your child, and what's more, I'm sure he will be the first of many."

By the end of February her daughter had been restored to her usual behavior and Carys was starting to wonder if new life was not budding at Sheridan Manor, inside her daughter's womb as well as in the fields yonder. Certainly, there had been no more discussions about courses coming when they were not wanted. Mother and daughter might well have another kind of discussion in the spring, one where Branwen told her she was to give her her first grandchild.

Her heart singing at the happy prospect, Carys went down the spiral staircase—and found herself face to face with James Mortimer. So close that they almost collided and fell to the floor, just like they had that night back in the summer.

What was he doing here?

He was the last person she'd expected to see, but that was hardly surprising. He'd been gone for eight months and they hadn't had word of his arrival. What had possessed him to come back in such a stealthy manner, as if he'd just gone for a drink at the village inn?

She took him in swiftly and was dismayed to find him looking rather worse for wear, as if he was recovering from an illness that had caused him to lose some weight. His jaw was covered with a dark stubble he'd not bothered to shave for several days, and his black eyes glimmered with a new intensity. He was still as forbidding as ever and her insides liquefied at his proximity.

"You're back! I thought we would never see you again." Shock made her sound more shrewish than she would have liked and his eyebrows shot to the roots of his hair. Oh, dear, she had offended him. The first words she had told him in months, and they had sounded like an accusation. "I only mean that you... You know what I meant."

"You learned to speak English," he replied instead of confirming that he did. Relief swept through her. He wasn't offended at her lack of manners, simply surprised to hear her speak his language, which made sense. He'd only ever heard her utter a handful of words in English before. "I thought I would never see the day."

"Yes. I did learn." She flushed. For some reason, it felt like a very private admission. The impression that she had made the effort just so that she could communicate with him when the time came flitted through her. Odd. She had never thought about it before, but now that he was in front of her, she could not help but wonder if that were not the case. "You've been gone for the best part of a year. It was great time I learn."

A gleam danced in his eyes and she guessed she had made a mistake in her use of English. She didn't care, because this gleam was one of the most fascinating things she had ever seen. It shouldn't have been possible to see eyes as dark as his light up, in the same way that ice would never catch on fire, or the sun would never shine at night, but she had not mistaken what she had seen. For the briefest of moments, his eyes *had* sparkled.

"How long have you been back?" she asked, instead of lingering on the pleasure it had given her to provoke a reaction, small as it was, in such an impassible man.

"I've just arrived, as you may have guessed." He gestured at his stubble and dusty clothes. "As a matter of fact, you're the first person I have seen."

James could barely talk for surprise. He had not expected Carys to be the first person he would bump into at Sheridan Manor. He'd been on his way to see Matthew, and inform him of his arrival, as was proper. And here she was, in front of him, looking lovelier than ever. She had lost the haunted look she'd had upon her arrival, as if she had finally found her place away from home. Speaking the language would help her fit in, undoubtedly.

His shock at hearing the English words in her mouth had been great. He had not dared hope she would have learned to speak his language while he'd been away. In fact, he had tried his best not to think about her at all.

With little success.

Frustration swelled within him. Not a vain man, James found himself deploring the bad timing of their meeting. Carys had never looked better, and he had never looked worse. In his travel clothes, with the beard on his jaw, and the gauntness he still had not recovered from, he would present a frightful sight, whereas she was as neat as a pin and as fresh as a rose in her sky blue gown.

Most ridiculously of all, now that he could finally converse with her, he was struck dumb. What a waste that was! He should start talking, now. But what could he say? He had no idea.

Joyous barks were heard in the distance, providing a welcome distraction. It appeared that someone else at Sheridan Manor knew he was back.

"Goldie!" He turned in time to catch the mighty dog bounding to him. She was followed by two younglings of a striking russet color who threw themselves against his legs when they saw the welcome their mother was giving him. "And who are these?" he asked, already knowing the answer.

They were none other than the pups that had been conceived in front of his very eyes that day by the river. He ruffled his dog's furry head affectionately. The encounter had borne fruit, as he'd suspected. Carys' lips quivered, confirming his suspicions.

"Meet Gweiadur and Rhwd," she said, laughter dancing in her voice. "The rest of the litter was given to a friend of Matthew's who visited one day but Eirwen had fallen in love with these two, and they were allowed to stay."

"Couldn't you have kept the ones called Blackie and Snowy, or some such?" he grumbled. How was he supposed to call the dogs with such impossible names? How was he supposed to *remember* them?

"You can call them Copper and Rust if you prefer. That's what everyone else does, but I kept the names Eirwen chose in Welsh." The laughter bubbling in her throat finally burst through. It was as charming as he remembered it, perhaps even more so, as he now knew what made her laugh. "We thought that given the parents' names, the metal theme was fitting."

It was. He had been struck by the fact that the two dogs bore matching names when she had introduced Silver to him. It had seemed significant somehow, a way of bringing their masters together.

"Copper and Rust it will have to be," he agreed. "Which one is which then?"

He reached out to the pup next to him. At the same time Carys' hand landed on the dog's head. His fingers covered hers. They both froze. He should have removed his hand. He did not. She could have stepped away. She did not. Time froze. His heartbeat increased.

"This one here is Rhwd," she breathed, staying very still.

"Rust, I'm guessing?" He sounded just as breathless.

"Yes."

Damn it all, he should definitely move. It was not like that day last summer when they had happened to land one on top of the other. This time it was not dark, everyone could see them, and the touching was deliberate. Instead of doing what he should, he got lost in Carys' eyes, two blue shimmering pools capable of drowning an unsuspecting man. Under his fingers he could feel her hand, so soft and small. Was she trembling? Or was it him? He could not be sure.

But something was happening.

"Ah James, there you are." Matthew's voice, calling from behind them, brought him back to the present. "I thought I'd seen your horse by the stable."

James lifted his hand from Carys' as unobtrusively as he could and turned to face him. With luck, he wouldn't have seen anything suspicious, just two people fussing over a dog.

"Yes. I just arrived."

Matthew crossed his arms over his chest, not looking best pleased. "It's been eight months. You could have sent word of your impending return, you know."

"I know. I didn't."

This blunt, uninformative answer elicited a snort. "Evidently. Come, you must be thirsty, and Branwen will be glad to see you. We've just finished eating, but I can ask for some food to be brought to you."

He nodded to Carys as well, and all three of them made their way to the solar. Branwen, who'd been writing a letter by the window, stood up at their entrance, a smile lighting her face.

"Look who I found in the bailey, Raven." At first, James had been surprised by the unusual nickname Matthew used for his wife but then he had told him that her name, Branwen, meant beautiful or white raven.

"James." She looked so pleased to see him, his heart gave a little jolt. It was almost as if he were more than the castle steward in her eyes. The thought moved him, because to him she was more than the mistress of the place as well. Brief as their acquaintance had been, she was the daughter-in-law he'd never thought to have. "Welcome back. I thought I heard a horse trot in earlier. But then nothing happened so I thought I was mistaken."

"You were not, my lady." He bowed to her. "I trust you're doing well?"

"Very well, thank you." She glanced at her husband, who automatically wrapped an arm around her waist to draw her closer to him. These two were still madly in love, he was glad to see.

"So tell us. How is your sister-in-law doing?" Matthew asked, while they all sat down.

"She'll be fine."

Both Matthew and Branwen arched their brow at this terse answer but James had no wish to discuss Margaret, now or ever. His stay under her roof had been an uncomfortable one. He had been unable to rid himself of the impression that she wanted more from him than mere comfort. The number of times she had alluded to the fact that they were now both widowed and alone had been far too high.

If truth be told, the whole affair had been a disaster.

He had meant to be gone a month, two at the most. In the end, he'd spent the best part of a year away from Sheridan Manor. First, he'd had to console Margaret, who had clung to him more desperately than he had anticipated in her grief. It had taken weeks to restore her to a semblance of sanity. Then, when he'd thought he could finally leave, he had been roped in the rebuilding her son Henry's barn. That had taken a while, as the villagers had not exactly been forthcoming with their help. James had the feeling that the man wasn't well-liked and it had not taken him long to see why. The lad was underhanded, lazy and incapable of keeping his hands to himself when in the presence of women.

Nevertheless, James had helped, for the sake of Henry's newly wedded wife. The poor woman, who was with child, deserved to have her supply of hay and grain kept dry in the winter. Life with a man like her husband would be hard enough. Once the work had been completed, he had gone to his parents, as planned, and found them both abed with a fever. He had nursed them back to health, which, given their age, had been a rather lengthy process. While he was there, he'd made sure to put everything in order for them, cutting a supply of wood that would see them through to spring.

At long last, he'd started his travel back to Sheridan Manor, stopping at Margaret's cottage for the night, as promised. In the morning, he'd been forced to deal with yet another complication. A severe chill he'd been unable to shake off had kept him in bed. To his intense surprise and annoyance, James had been incapacitated for over three weeks.

The unexpected delay had taken its toll on his mood. Then, as if all that had not been enough, snow had made his travel back home slower than he would have liked.

"I'm glad to be back," he concluded, putting an end to that discussion. He simply wanted to put the whole episode behind him. "I confess that I regretted not being at Sheridan Manor to celebrate Christmas."

"I imagine you would have felt rather lonely."

"I did. All the people I care about are here."

As he spoke he glanced over at Carys, who had settled herself in a corner of the room, and was working on embroidering a shift. It looked to be exquisite work, an utter extravagance for a garment destined to be hidden from view. James knew of few people who would be willing to lavish such effort on something no one would ever see. Too many of his acquaintances did things because they wanted to impress others. Carys, on the contrary, was only trying to please herself, and surround herself with beautiful things.

Was the shift she was wearing right now as lavishly decorated? One way of getting an answer would be to lift her skirt, he supposed, and examine the hem. How low did the decoration he could see peeking above the bodice of her blue gown go? Was the whole of her shift covered in leaves and flowers? Dare he undress her to find out?

He shook his head and bit into the pie Matthew had asked a servant to bring him. What was wrong with him? He'd barely been back a moment, and he was already thinking about Carys in inappropriate terms.

"Have I missed something here?" he asked once his composure had been restored. Thank God they were sitting down and no one had noticed the bulge in his hose.

"No. Apart from Carys and Eirwen having started to speak English. They are doing well."

Yes, he knew that already, but he didn't say so. For a reason he could not fathom, he didn't want anyone to know he'd stopped to talk to Carys before he'd gone to see them. It was ridiculous. After all, it was not as if they had done anything forbidden, and Matthew had seen them together anyway.

"I am pleased. It will be easier for everyone," he commented. "I saw my Goldie gave birth to her first litter."

"Yes." Branwen smiled. "We suspect Silver to be the father."

James didn't say anything. He didn't want to have to explain why he knew for certain Silver was the father. He couldn't, however, stop himself from stealing a glance at Carys. She was working very hard at untangling a thread that had somehow become knotted on itself. A most unexpected mishap to happen to such a talented embroiderer. Was she, like him, remembering the day by the river when they had seen the dogs? Perhaps, too, the night back in June when she had fallen on him?

Was that the reason for her unrest?

"What about you, James?" Matthew asked roundly. "Forgive me for saying as much, but you look as if you've not been well."

"That's because I haven't. But I should be over the worst now."

"Oh, dear." Branwen sounded full of concern. "I hope you don't intend to overtax yourself now that you're back."

"I won't." James stood up more abruptly than he'd intended. "If you will excuse me, however, I will go and see that everything is in order. I've been away for too long."

Yes, too long, but not long enough to forget the Welsh woman doing her best to blend into the background.

Chapter Four

T he robin had fluffed up his feathers and was cleaning himself thoroughly, spreading his wings, lifting his tail, shaking his head. His little inflated body was twice its usual size, and almost perfectly round. He was so beautiful. Carys smiled to herself. Robins had always been her favorite birds. She would have liked nothing more than to scoop him up in her palm and cradle his softness in her palms. He would weigh nothing, and be as fragile as newly fallen snow.

Was everything that was good in life as fleeting and delicate? Love certainly seemed to be. She and her husband had loved one another fiercely, and yet there was nothing left of it now. The only proof there had ever been a man called Dewi ab Anarawd lived in her memory, where no one could see it.

The bird shook himself one last time and let out a contented chirp. She tilted her head, unable to detach her gaze from him.

"Now, what has you so fascinated, I wonder?"

Carys let out a little gasp when the question reached her from behind. James. She had still not accustomed herself to him being back—or that she could understand him. All those months ago she had thought his way of talking particularly gruff. She could see now that it was in fact simply due to his deep voice.

"The bird, here, on the—"

Before she could finish the sentence, the robin had flown away. Carys followed him with her gaze for as long as she could. Where was he going? To the forest yonder or farther away? Did he mean to reach the sea? Lucky him.

"The robin that was here you mean?" James asked, drawing to her side.

"Yes." She was delighted by the piece of information. She had not known the English name for the bird, and loved that it was the same as it was Welsh. *Robin goch*. Red robin. It would be one less word to remember. "I love robins."

"Why?"

He sounded nonplussed that anyone could express such a sentiment, and perhaps it was foolish to have a favorite bird. Because when she wanted to explain what the attraction was she discovered that she had no idea why that was exactly. She had always liked them, ever since she was a child and she'd not thought she would ever have to justify her decision to anyone.

"I don't know." What could she say? "They are so funny, don't you think?. Round and lovely."

"I suppose so." He didn't sound convinced but eager not to contradict her. It made her smile.

James watched Carys look back in the direction where the little robin had flown. There was a look of wonder on her face, as if she had just seen an angel. It puzzled him. How could the sight of a bird have sent her into such a reverie? How many robins, wrens or sparrows had he seen in his life, without ever thinking anything of it? Her capacity to find beauty and joy in the simplest things amazed him. Only the day before he had seen her eyes light up when Silver had run up to her. Even though he imagined she saw the dog every day of her life, you could have sworn she'd been reunited with a long-lost friend. Everything she did was done with the same enthusiasm. She always ate with relish, laughed as if she had no care in the world, walked as if she were heading for a place where untold delights awaited her.

Next to her he felt oddly constrained, dull.

Odd, because as a young man, he had never thought of himself in that way. True, he had never been the most outspoken of men, but then Joanne had changed him, for the better. During their marriage, he'd been able to fight his natural tendency to be withdrawn. Since her death, he had kept himself to himself, and not worried about how he appeared to others. But perhaps now that he'd lost what little passion she'd managed to spark in him he had become a hollow husk of a man.

It was not a pleasing thought.

"I've never seen the sea," Carys said, bringing him back to the present. "Dewi and I said we would go together but we never did."

"Dewi?"

She flushed, looking caught out. It was not the first time he'd heard her express her inner feelings out loud. In fact, it was one of the many things he liked about her. She was never ashamed of what she thought, so much so that she allowed everyone to hear it.

"My late husband. He promised me he would take me there one day. We never made the effort to organize the outing, though, thinking we could go any time we wanted. And we could have. Only, we didn't, and in the end, he died without having seen it. I wish it had been different, because it would have taken little effort to actually go."

The confession, so simple, so heartfelt, moved him. He, too, had planned to do things with Joanne, things he had not been able to find the courage to do without her. His heart went to Carys because he understood exactly what she meant. These little things had a way of being swallowed by life's hectic pace. You promised yourself to do something, but because it was unimportant or seemed easy to organize, you put them to one side, for a moment when you had nothing better to do.

And then one day, before you knew it, it was too late.

"The sea is not so far from here," he told her, barely resisting the urge to take her hand in his. "Tomorrow, I'll take you there."

Tomorrow. There would be no delay, no excuses, no chance to refuse. Suddenly nothing seemed more important that this little thing. Because it was with Carys.

When she looked up at him, her blue eyes were sparkling, just like the surface of the sea when the sun reflected over it. His breath caught in his chest. Beautiful.

"Would you really? Oh, I would love that."

Yes, he would take her there. Nothing would stop him, if it was going to give her such pleasure. He would take her there and watch the wonder on her face.

"I'll come to find you tomorrow. Be ready at dawn."

"There it is, between the trees."

Carys frowned and peered into the distance. "Are you certain this is it?"

"I am." James laughed at her obvious discomfiture. "Let me guess. You expected something more spectacular."

There was no denying it. All she could see was a gray band floating ahead of them, barely distinguishable from the horizon, framed by slightly disheveled trees. This first glimpse was underwhelming to say the least. *This* was the sea? She had spent so long dreaming about this moment that she could not help feeling somewhat deflated. Perhaps she could have spared herself the trouble of coming all this way.

"Wait," James said, sensing her disappointment. "Give it a second chance. Sometimes first impressions are misleading. We are still some distance away but you might think differently once you get nearer and see it for what it really is."

"Are you still talking about the sea?" she muttered.

He cocked his head and gave her a blinding smile, the likes of which she had never thought to see on his face. It transformed him. She didn't have time to bask in it, however, because then he asked, "Of course. What else would I be talking about?"

Go drapia! She'd spoken aloud again. Would she never get rid of this silly habit of hers? Since he'd heard her, she decided to brazen it out. "I thought perhaps you would be talking about yourself?"

"Me?" He arched a brow in surprise.

"Well, you are rather gruff on first acquaintance, wouldn't you say? Or even on second or third."

"I don't know, I... Am I?"

He sounded so genuinely put out that she regretted the tease. He hadn't been gruff toward her, exactly. Most of the impression might have been due to the fact that he looked so forbidding in black—and that they hadn't been able to understand one another. Because now that she knew him, she saw that he was remarkably even-tempered for such a virile man.

"It wasn't so bad," she soothed. "I expect it was inevitable I should think you gruff when I didn't understand what you were telling me."

"No, it wasn't inevitable. Words are one thing, attitude another. I hope I didn't give you the impression I wanted to rip your head off."

Rip her head off? She laughed out loud at the unlikely

image. She doubted anything would rile James Mortimer so much as to make him lash out at someone. He simply didn't seem to be the kind of man who would allow his temper to overrule him thus.

"Oh, no. Nothing so dramatic as that," she assured him. He nodded, still looking less than pleased. Why had she thought to tease him? How had she not guessed a man as serious as he was wouldn't respond well to it? "Shall we?" she asked, hoping to put an end to the moment. "I can't wait to get a closer look at the sea."

They walked on. When she had confessed not to be a skilled rider, James had made sure to saddle for her the mount she had used to come from Wales. She was an old mare with a placid disposition, nothing like the spirited stallion—boasting a shiny black coat, naturally—that he'd chosen for himself. Not having to worry about falling down allowed Carys to relax and focus on the landscape around them. And it was beautiful, a succession of rolling hills and gnarled old trees. The air was scented with the proximity of the sea, she guessed, and she inhaled the brine deeply. It certainly smelled different, sharper than what she was used to. After having followed a narrow track through the woods, they came to a bend—and there it was.

The mare stopped.

Carys gaped.

The sea sparkled.

James chuckled.

"Not so disappointed now, I see," he drawled.

She didn't turn to him when she answered on a breath. "No."

How could she be? She had never seen anything more beautiful. Even though she had imagined this moment many times, the reality surpassed her imagination. Would she have been as struck had it not been a sunny day and the sea not sparkled so, she wondered?

Yes. Somehow, she was certain that even under leaden skies, the view would have taken her breath away.

"Come," James said quietly. "We need to get closer. I know the best place to go."

After a short ride down gentle slopes, they finally reached their destination. They hitched the horses to a cluster of trees that seemed made for that purpose and walked toward the edge of the water, which was coming and retreating rhythmically, creating a sort of foam as it did. Was it supposed to do that? Carys had never seen anything like it. One glance at James made it clear he was unconcerned. Perhaps everything was as it should be. Feeling somewhat ridiculous at her lack of knowledge, she edged closer.

"It's nothing like the lake near the village," she observed under her breath.

"No. I can imagine. It will be much bigger."

"Yes. And rather daunting. Peaceful. Unfamiliar. Soothing."

"All this?"

"All this. And more."

He seemed delighted by her reaction, which puzzled her. What had she done save give her honest opinion? But now that she thought of it, he always seemed to enjoy watching her enjoy something. Perhaps because his own reactions were so subdued, he liked seeing someone experience things to the full? It would make sense. Well, if he enjoyed that, he had definitely come to the right person. Carys was incapable of keeping her reactions, be they good or bad, to herself. She wore her heart on her sleeve and she was not afraid to let her emotions show, especially delight. Expressing them out loud seemed to allow her to feel them with more intensity.

"Do you want to dip your feet in?" James suggested when

she was about to ask if they could get even closer. "It would be a pity to have come all this way and not even enjoy the feel of the water against your skin, don't you think?"

Yes, it would be.

James wanted Carys to make the most of the moment, not only for her sake, but for his also. He would derive even more pleasure from watching her than he would from feeling the cool water snake around his ankles. After all, it was nothing new to him. But he knew she would love it.

"Is it safe? I don't know how to swim," she admitted with a delicious blush.

"You won't need to. The water is very shallow for several yards around here," he explained, trying not to dwell on how that blush became her. It made it impossible to look anywhere else but at her beautiful face. "It's perfectly safe."

"Can you swim?"

"Yes. So there is nothing to fear, I'll catch you if you slip." He would even enjoy it. "I will come in the water with you, so you can hold on to my arm if you need to."

That seemed to decide her. Without further ado, she sat down to remove her shoes and stockings. The gesture was so artless, it denoted such enthusiasm, he felt something tighten inside him. What that might be, he wasn't sure but he suspected it might be joy. The simple joy of being with someone who enjoyed what life had to offer. After having been alone for so long, after having almost died, that was exactly what he needed.

But even if it hadn't been, he could not have prevented himself from wanting to be with Carys. He'd been attracted to her from the start, and he was more attracted to her than ever, which was little wonder.

How could she appear so youthful with two grown daughters, he asked himself for the hundredth time? Her face was perfection, her hair the most extraordinary color. He could tell it had been a rich auburn when she was younger. But the silver strands time had woven through it, instead of being spread throughout, as it was in other people, himself included, were focused in two wide streaks either side of her head. They followed the shell of her ear, starting at her temple, and running all the way to the end of the long locks, which hung in soft waves over her shoulders. The effect was striking, unlike anything he had ever seen.

Was it enough to explain the fascination she exerted over him? No. But combined with her smile, the sparkle in her eyes, her boundless enthusiasm and the lilting accent giving her every declaration an entrancing quality, it was more than enough.

Without ceremony, she bunched her skirts in one hand and walked toward the lapping waves. As spring was still a few weeks away, he knew the water would be cold. The sea was also rather agitated that morning, but he didn't mention anything, since it was safe, as he'd said. There was no point in worrying her for nothing.

"Are you not waiting for me then?" he asked, as he started to remove his boots.

"No. You're taking forever, and I'm impa—" She let out a little shriek when the first wave hit her toes.

"Cold?" he asked, amused.

"Yes. And tickly," she replied, retreating hastily. As she did so, she wavered, unused to the sensation of having sand being sucked from under her feet. Fortunately, he had reached her by then and he steadied her with an arm about the waist.

"Here. I told you I would not let you fall."

"*Diolch.*" She automatically thanked him in Welsh.

"What should I answer to this, I wonder?" he asked, leaning in to speak in her ear.

"*A chroeso.*"

Her voice was barely above a whisper. He did his best to

repeat the words as faithfully as he could and was rewarded with a blinding smile. "*Da iawn*! Well done."

"My first words in Welsh," James confided. Only for her would he have attempted such a thing. He'd heard enough of the language to see it would not be easily mastered.

"Thank you, I had guessed as much." There was mirth in her voice but no mockery. "It seems we have both experienced something new today."

"It would appear so. Shall we carry on?"

"Yes. I'm not one for giving up so easily."

No. He didn't think she would be.

Hand in hand, they walked back to the edge of the water and only stopped when their feet were completely covered by the churning sea. It was as cold as he had feared, but not for all the gold in the world would he have wished himself anywhere else.

"Is it always thus?" Carys asked, lifting her head to him. "Does the water always go back and forth in that manner, I mean?"

She looked cautious, as if fearing he would think her silly for not knowing but eager to have an answer nonetheless. Of course, if she had never seen the sea before, she would be surprised by the motion. How had he not thought?

He nodded. "Yes. It never stops, never for a moment. Not only that, but it expands. It is low tide now, but do you see those rocks next to where we tethered the horses? The water will slowly creep up to them over the course of the afternoon. Then it will start retreating back to the place it is now, and the same thing will happen again at night. It does this twice a day, every day."

"That's incredible."

"Yes. It's a movement that's as old as time."

Back and forth. Retreating then plunging in again.

Suddenly the words made him think of another such movement that had been part of people's lives since the dawn of humanity. How long since he had experienced the joy of being one with a woman, of moving inside her and getting lost in the moment? Too long. But, as much as he missed it, he knew why he didn't indulge in the pleasure of it. It was not just that few women piqued his interest, though that was certainly one reason. But the act was not without consequence. Children were created during such joinings, and then their parents had to watch as they died.

James had been through that awful pain four times already. Once would have been once too many, four was just plain cruelty. He could not bear the idea of seeing a child of his loins die ever again. Much better to keep his urges in check. And mercifully, there were other ways to get—and give pleasure.

"I want to go a bit further."

"Yes."

So did he. But he didn't think they were talking about the same thing.

Carys could not help a shriek when a wave, more forceful than the others, crashed against her legs, splashing her all the way to her knees. Not only was the sea going back and forth, but it was also unpredictable. It seemed that some waves were stronger than others, and she'd been caught out.

"Will you look at that!" She giggled, gesturing at her dress. "I'm all wet!"

James gave her an odd look, one that was too intense by far, considering what they were discussing.

"You are paddling in the sea, that will be why," he said before she could make sense of it. "Doing certain things will make you wet, there's no avoiding it. It's not always a bad thing, though."

Everything within her tightened, or loosened, she wasn't quite sure which. Was he... had he just alluded to—

Another wave crashed against her legs. This time she didn't do anything to try and avoid it, she didn't shriek. In fact she barely noticed it, so lost was she trying to puzzle out James' words and containing the wild beating of her heart.

After a long while, he cleared his throat. "The tide's coming in, that's why the waves are coming with more force. I'd better get you away from here," he said softly. "Or you'll end up completely drenched."

She couldn't nod; she couldn't speak. All she knew was that she was drenched already, only not in the way he meant. Dear God, what had just happened? Nothing. And yet she felt as breathless as if James had just kissed her senseless.

They retrieved their shoes in silence and made their way back to the blanket he'd spread on the sand earlier.

Carys sat down and lifted her head up to the sun while her dress and feet dried, trying to regain her composure. The peaceful setting helped. The bay curved gently on either side of them, and she could distinguish various shades of green, gray and blue in the water, depending on how the sunlight hit the surface. No one was around, and it looked as if the place had been created for them, like the perfect cocoon.

"How long were you married?"

She stilled as the question hit her, as unexpected as the waves had been earlier. Why did James want to know? And why now?

"Almost twelve years."

"Was it a happy marriage?"

"Yes. Dewi and I got married when we were both seventeen, and we were deeply in love." She gave a wistful smile. It had been love at first sight between the two of them. Her friends had warned her that such an attraction would fade as quickly as it had come, but it had not. It had only transformed into something deeper and more meaningful. Had he not died so prematurely, they would still be happy today, she had no doubt in her mind. "He used to joke that my parents had chosen my name well."

"How so?"

Carys blinked. Of course, not speaking Welsh, he wouldn't know what her name meant. And now she would have to spell it out. Why hadn't she kept her mouth shut?

"It can be translated as 'beloved' in your language," she explained, reddening a little. "And he kept saying that, as his wife, I certainly was loved."

James pierced her with one of the intense stares she had grown to love. "It's a beautiful name, and a beautiful sentiment. I can understand why you were happy married to such a man."

She swallowed hard. Yes, she had been more than happy with Dewi, but it felt like so long ago now. Eighteen years, to be precise, which was to say that she had spent much longer being a widow than a married woman. Her memories of him had started to fade, and there was no way to stop it. In a few years' time, she might not remember the way he'd looked when passion stirred him or the sound of his voice. The thought was so depressing that she asked James a question of her own, eager to move the focus away from memories of her life with Dewi.

"What about you?" She knew from Branwen that he was a widower, too, but she didn't know much more.

He sighed and lay on the blanket, next to her. For a moment she thought he would not answer but then he started to talk, his eyes on the sky above, his voice flat.

"I met my wife, Joanne, when I was eighteen. Just like you with Dewi, I knew immediately she would be the woman I would marry, and she would make me a happy man. And for almost twenty years, she did. I woke up every morning thinking I had been right to follow my instinct."

Carys could not help a smile because she remembered that feeling all too well. The certainty of being with the person you were meant to be with, the comfort it brought you, the happiness. As soon as she had met Dewi, she'd known they were destined to be together and every day she had thanked her lucky stars she had not listened to the people who had tried to caution her against a hasty decision. Sometimes your heart *did* know better and you were rewarded for following it.

She stole a glance at James, who was still looking at the sky. What she felt when she was with him was different to what she had felt with her husband, but no less potent. The only difference was, she wasn't sure where it would lead. With Dewi, she had not asked herself any questions. They would marry and have a family together. That was what young people did, the only satisfying way forward she could see. But now... A woman her age, with two grown daughters, could do what she wanted. Supposing she knew what it was she wanted, of course. Right now, she wasn't sure.

Confused, she decided to lie down, like James. High above, a cloud was hurrying toward the sun, pushed by the sea breeze. Would it run past it, dimming its brilliance for a moment?

"Do you have any children?" she asked.

There was a long pause. Then two words, terrible. "Not anymore."

After that there was nothing to say.

When she moved, the sand under the blanket shifted, allowing her to mold her body into a soft cocoon. This was delicious, so delicious that after a moment she feared she would fall asleep. Not wanting to waste her first day at the sea sleeping, Carys stood back up, intent on returning to the edge of the water, which had indeed come closer during their discussion.

As she placed her foot down, a small bolt of pain shot through her foot. What was that? And how had she not felt it before?

"Ow, I think I must have stepped on something sharp earlier," she said, sitting back down.

"Probably a broken shell. It can happen all too easily on sand. Let me see."

Without waiting for her agreement, James lifted her foot up for inspection. She thought perhaps she should protest but she did not. Where was the harm in it? As he examined her foot she watched him. His dark eyes were focused, his jaw set. There was something about a man who didn't smile, she decided. It made his demeanor even more manly. Irresistible.

"Yes, there is a cut, here." His finger brushed a spot just below her big toe. Had she been ticklish she might have wiggled away. As she was not, she simply enjoyed the caress. "It's not very big. You likely didn't feel it earlier because of the cold of the sea. Not to worry, it should heal easily enough."

While he was speaking, his hand had started to creep up on her leg. His finger was no longer on the cut but halfway up her calf, and showing no sign of stopping.

"What are you doing?" she croaked, unable to do as she ought and snatch her leg away.

"Touching you."

Yes, well, this much she could feel. What she was wondering was why. "You shouldn't be doing that."

The mouth that never smiled curled up at the corner. "You're right. I should be licking you."

With those shocking words, James brought her feet to his mouth and kissed the bone on her ankle. Carys inhaled sharply. Still, she didn't move, and the lips slid upward slowly, trailing a path of fire along her calf. What was the man doing? And why was she not protesting? Because it felt too good, that was why.

Heavenly.

"Mm, you taste of salt and sun-warmed skin," he growled. "Let me feast on the rest of you."

Possibly because no one had ever demanded such a thing from her, she didn't respond. What could she have said anyway?

Yes, the answer that had immediately come to mind, was too scandalous by far. *No,* too absurd, and a lie. She did want him to feast on her. *You're not serious* would be too naïve, because there was no mistaking his intent. He had spoken in earnest. *Please* could surely be—

In her confusion, Carys left it too long and he took her silence for agreement. Placing a hand on her shoulder, he nudged her backward until she was lying on the blanket once more. It seemed he would have her comfortable while he explored her body.

"Yes. Salt. Sun. Cream. Honey. Silk. Woman." Each word was punctuated by a kiss. Each kiss took him closer to the place between her thighs that felt impossibly swollen. Soon he would reach it and see how wet she was. There would be no hiding it. Anticipation was coursing through her veins. If he didn't stop he would get to taste the desire dripping from her.

He didn't stop.

Her dress and shift were gathered up and the sea breeze came to tease her intimate folds. There was no doubting this was what he intended to kiss next. Her whole body tensed. How long had it been since a man had not pleasured her thus?

Too long.

The first lick made her eyes roll into the back of her head. There was nothing tentative about it. James took his time and, very slowly, very deliberately, used the flat of his tongue to trace a path from the bottom to the top of her womanly seam. When he reached the place at the apex of her thighs he kissed it and groaned, like a man grateful to have been allowed his favorite treat.

What was he doing to her? No sooner had he started pleasuring her than he had reduced her to a panting, squirming mess. Carys made sounds she hadn't known she could make, sounds she wasn't even sure were human. But how could she do otherwise? His tongue, his warm, wicked, delicious, skilled tongue was everywhere at once. Just when she thought his caresses could not get more decadent, he brought it lower, between her buttocks, and started teasing a part of her no one had ever touched before, much less licked.

She bucked so hard she knocked him on the chin.

"Easy, love," he rasped, placing his hands on her hip bones to hold her in place. "You don't want to hurt me, not now, not before I have finished what I'm doing."

"But what you're doing is—"

"Delicious. You will have noticed, I hope."

Oh, yes, she had. Why did he think she had almost snapped her spine in two trying to cope with the sensations?

Just when she thought he could not do anything more scandalous, he did just that. Putting his hands under her knees, he lifted her buttocks high in the air. Carys found herself folded in two, totally exposed to his gaze and mouth—and just as aroused as she was mortified. In that shocking position, he would have access to all her intimate parts. The way his eyes gleamed told her it had been exactly his intention.

"So beautiful." His voice was darker than it had ever been. A shiver went up her spine. "Ask me to carry on, Carys. Beg me to lick you, everywhere, and make you come."

"I-I could not," she whimpered. Was he mad? She would never be able to utter such shameless words, or demand anyone did such a thing.

"Do it in Welsh, if you must. But I won't start again until you beg me."

She tried to move, and found that she could not. His hold was as unbreakable as iron chains, even if it didn't hurt. Being at his mercy was sending her heart in a flurry and setting her bones on fire. And so she did beg. "Please, James."

The wretched man only smiled. She couldn't help a groan. Oh, *now* he was smiling! "Not good enough, sweeting."

Sweeting? How could he use such a tender endearment considering what he had done to her, what he wanted to make her say, and the way he was holding her? He should be calling her rude names.

True to his words, he did not resume his attentions, merely brought his face closer to her exposed womanhood and gave a growl low in his throat.

"Please, Carys. Ask me to lick you. I'm about to expire from need."

He was dying? What should she be saying?

"Well, lick me, damn you! Finish what you started. I need your tongue, everywhere, I need to come!"

The words exploded out of her, the most shocking thing she had said in her life. But as soon as she closed her mouth she understood why he had wanted her to beg him. Because as the command left her lips, a flush of moisture rushed between her thighs. She had been aroused a moment ago, she was now positively weeping with need.

Please, put an end to the torture.

"It will be my pleasure," he said darkly before lowering his head.

His tongue speared straight into her, and heat exploded inside Carys' skull. He circled her opening slowly, once, twice, a third time with the tip of his tongue. No! This was too delicate, she was too far gone for such teasing. She sank her fingers into his hair to indicate she needed him to be more forceful.

He understood and complied only too readily.

After that she barely knew what he was doing. Pleasure blended into one huge mass of sensations, each more bewildering than the last. Her lower body was numbed, or too sensitive to touch, she wasn't sure quite which. Perhaps both. Wicked fingers soon joined the dance of his tongue and lips, and at long last, she soared straight out of her body.

Her release was so strong she lost the ability to breathe.

James held her in position for a long moment, murmuring soothing words against her flesh, then lowered her back to the blanket.

"Thank you."

She wasn't sure why she was thanking him, and indeed it was a ridiculous thing to say after what had happened, but he tilted his head as if he didn't see anything odd in it. "*A chroeso.*"

And then, very deliberately, his eyes never leaving hers, he licked his lips.

Carys closed her eyes.

While she tried to bring her breathing back to normal, James covered her, rearranging her shift and dress until she was decent again. Reality came back, one sense at a time. The sound of the waves, the cry of the seagulls, the heat of the sun started to register once more.

When she opened her eyes again, James was gazing at her with piercing black eyes. Her heart skipped a beat. Had she really thought him impassible once? That he did not express his every feeling did not mean he did not feel them as strongly as she did. The fire burning in him right now was all too obvious.

"Don't look at me," she whimpered.

"I will look at you if I wish. You're the most—" She stopped him with an arched brow. He could not be saying she was the most beautiful woman he had ever seen. That could not be, and after the intimacy they had just shared she would not bear to hear such an outrageous lie. A slow smile bloomed on his lips, the sensual lips which only moments ago had been devouring her as if he had never had a woman in his arms before. He had acted like a man acknowledging a challenge and raising to it with dizzying enthusiasm. "You're the most exquisite woman I've ever tasted."

"Oh!"

The impossible man, giving impossibly shocking compliments! But how could she take issue with what he'd said? She knew full well there were more attractive women around but she had no idea how she tasted, did she? He might be telling the truth, as he knew it. Which hardly helped her hold on to her composure. Who praised women on the taste of their... of their—

"Come." James handed his hand out to her, mercifully putting an end to the awkwardness. "I am parched and I'm sure you could do with a drink too. There's a wineskin of ale in my horse's saddlebag."

This return to normality after such an earth-shattering moment could have offended her. In fact, it was what she needed not to dissolve in embarrassment. By behaving as if he'd not just used her body in the most forbidden fashion, he was allowing her not to dwell on it. And she *was* parched, perhaps because of all the panting, and the moaning, and the screaming. Oh, the screaming. She was certain she had never been quite that vocal with Dewi. But then again, she had been a different woman back then, young and relatively untried. If growing older did one thing for you, it was give you more confidence and the ability to stop worrying about what people might think.

Besides, she was certain James had liked hearing her express her enjoyment.

Accepting his hand, she stood up. But after her powerful release, her legs were too shaky to support her, especially on such an unstable surface. She stumbled and fell into his arms.

"Careful, sweeting. Feeling your delectable body against mine might give me ideas."

It was only then she realized he had not taken his pleasure. He had lapped at her in a frenzy of lust, brought her to ecstasy and sounded as if he'd thoroughly enjoyed it, but he had not reached his release, or even given himself as much as one stroke.

"You... Would you like me to... You didn't—"

"Hush." The expression on his face changed. He looked almost annoyed, an unexpected reaction, Carys thought. "Worry not about me."

She wasn't worried, exactly, but she couldn't help but wonder at it. What man would refuse her offer? A man who did not truly desire her, that was who.

"You do not want me then?" she said dejectedly. Perhaps he did not, or at least not enough to take her, and that was why he hadn't liked her asking if she could bring him release.

Her heart sank.

You do not want me then?

James blinked. Had the woman really asked him that after he had pleasured her to within an inch of her life and his control? Couldn't she see the desire burning in his eyes? Never had he been so consumed with the need to take and plunder a woman's body. Which was precisely why he could not surrender. He was too far gone, he wouldn't be able to stop himself from spilling inside her if he took her now, and nothing else than this complete possession would satisfy him.

He had not for a moment considered taking himself in hand to release the desire boiling in his spine, already knowing that it would feel hollow after what they had shared. He wanted all of Carys and would not accept less.

The taste of her lingered on his tongue, the scent of her teased his nostrils, the feel of her writhing in his arms already haunted his memory. So sweet, so maddening, so soft. So perfect.

But because of his restraint, she was worried he did not find her desirable. He could not let her think such a thing.

"Of course, I—"

He was prevented from telling her just how much he wanted her by a series of shrieks coming from behind the dunes. Women and children, by the sound of things, at least a dozen. He felt Carys tense against him and he knew what she would be thinking. Barely a moment ago, she'd been lying on the sand, spread open, and he'd been lapping at her. They could have been seen in that most intimate position. They had almost been.

He tightened his hold around her and murmured in her ear. "It's all right. No one can know what we just did."

She didn't seem convinced and, in truth, she did look flushed and thoroughly ravished. Perhaps the women would venture a guess as to what they had just done. Well, what of it? Far from feeling shame, pride swelled within him. *He* had been the one giving Carys that glow. It was the most satisfying thing he had done in years.

Rolling up the blanket, he led her toward the trees. He already knew he would place that blanket on his bed tonight and keep it there from now on, as a reminder of the moment they had shared this afternoon.

"Wait here, I'll get the drink."

As he reached the horses, a little boy's head appeared above the crest of the nearest dune. His eyes lit up when he saw the sea and he started to run to it. Carried forward by the momentum, unable to stop himself on the down slope, he went head over heels, rolling until he came to a stop at Carys' feet. She laughed and helped him up, brushing sand from his hair and clothes with motherly affection.

"That's what comes from rushing, you little—" He did not understand the word she used and guessed it would have been the Welsh for rascal, or something similar. A smile tugged at his lips. "I understand why you did though. The sea is wonderful, is it not? Are you going for a swim?"

"Get away from the woman, Georgie!" a tall woman, presumably his mother, cried out, once she had made it down the dune in a more controlled manner.

"It's all right," Carys gave the little boy a grin. "He didn't bother me in the least, I assure—"

"Let go of him, you Welsh barbarian!"

"You have nothing to do here."

"Don't even think of touching our children!"

The women, all four of them, surrounded Carys, distrust etched on their faces. It was clear they had identified her as an enemy and, confident in their numeric superiority, were about to unleash their venom onto her. Venom or even possibly physical violence.

James was behind them in the blink of an eye.

"Is there a problem here?" he asked in his best menacing voice, hinting that if there was, he would be all too happy to solve it, but in a manner that might not meet their approval.

The women, who obviously had not seen him amongst the horses and trees, yelped at the interruption. Then the tall one, recognizing him for an Englishman from his speech, stepped forward, hope gleaming in her eyes at the thought of having met an ally.

"Oh, sir, this woman is—"

"This woman is helping your son putting himself to rights after his fall," he cut in before she could utter the insult already on her lips. "Do you have a problem with that? Wouldn't you have done the same?"

"But she's Welsh!"

"Yes, she is." This flat, unemotional confirmation seemed to puzzle the woman. She had clearly expected him to agree that Carys was therefore unsuitable to be in the vicinity of young children, in the same way a ferocious ogre would be. He waited. When no other argument was brought forward, he asked: "Are you familiar with Lord Sheridan?"

She arched a brow. "Of course."

James had guessed she would be. Everyone around here knew Connor Hunter. He commanded respect, but more importantly, he was well-liked and acknowledged as a just and generous lord.

"Well, his brother, Matthew, is married to this woman's daughter. Welsh as she may be, Branwen ferch Gethin is effectively the new mistress of the place, and a good woman. I don't think the people at Sheridan Manor would like to hear anyone was stirring trouble about her mother. They might well find themselves having to answer for their actions to her husband and Lord Sheridan himself."

The women recoiled like frightened birds and he knew he had won. They would leave Carys alone if they ever crossed paths with her again.

"There will be no trouble from us, sir," a blonde one said, grabbing her tall friend by the elbow as if to urge her to stay silent. "We were only taking the children to the beach, as you can see."

"Yes. Don't let us stop you then."

They hurried away, muttering amongst themselves.

James turned to Carys, who looked more forlorn than he had ever seen her. Damn the women for making her feel this way! She was the happiest, most carefree, loving woman he knew and she'd been made to feel a monster for coming to a child's rescue. That was bad enough, but their unwarranted attack had wiped the glow from her face, the one he'd been so proud to see only a moment ago.

Now when she remembered her first outing to the sea, she might not think of the water lapping at her toes, or the waves of pleasure crashing through her body when he had devoured her. She might think back to the vile women who'd treated her like dirt. He almost ran to them to ram their words back into their throats.

"Carys, I'm—"

"Shall we?" she cut in, her voice but a whisper. "I would like to reach Sheridan Manor before nightfall."

Chapter Five

"Why did you take my defense?"

It was only when they reached the cover of the trees that Carys found the courage to ask the question. She had been grateful to see him spring to her aid so promptly, but surprised nonetheless.

James stared at her, looking more than a little bit offended. "Do I really need to explain? Weren't my reasons clear enough?"

"Yes, they were." The women had been awful toward her, and might well have turned violent, safe in the knowledge no one could see them on the deserted beach. "But I think there's something else."

There had been an unusual intent in his eyes. It could have been due to what had just happened between them on the blanket, of course, but she suspected he was hiding something from her. There had been something possessive, almost feral in his attitude. It would have been hard to justify coming from anyone else. Coming from a man as controlled and quiet as he was, it was almost worrying. So what was it? Did he know the women? Did he have a score to settle with them? Say what he might, there had been more to his reaction than mere outrage on her behalf.

Though he didn't answer, Carys didn't insist. She knew him well enough to guess he would talk when he was ready, since her question was a reasonable one.

"You're right," he sighed eventually, proving her right. "I guess I cannot stand by and watch anyone being mocked because of their origins when I have suffered from the same prejudice myself."

This was the last thing she had expected to hear. Who had dared mock a man like him? "You? But you're not Welsh, are you?"

"No. I think we have safely established that by now." He gave a small smile. Indeed they had. "But you will have noticed I am darker than most."

She had, but stupidly she had attributed it to the fact that he was English, and therefore different to the men she was used to. Now she felt rather silly because, come to think of it, the people she had met here were indistinguishable from the ones she had left behind in Wales. Except James Mortimer. She had focused so much on how unsettled she felt in his presence that she had failed to see that the effect was not simply due to his dour countenance and black clothing. He was, just as he'd said, darker than most. His eyes, his hair, his skin.

He *did* stand out. Like a foreigner.

"What are you then? You sound very English to me, just like Matthew."

"Oh, I am English, only... my father wasn't. My real father, I mean. Not the one I visited in the winter, who lives with my mother, as her husband. I owe my coloring to the man who sired me. Not many people would dare raise the issue now that I'm a grown man, but as a child, I suffered my share of insults because of it. It was obvious when one saw me next to my older, blond siblings that, not only was I not of my fair father's getting, but also from a different origin. It made for an easy target."

He stared into the distance, as if lost in unpleasant memories of that time. Carys' chest tightened at the idea of James being taunted and perhaps hurt as a young boy. It was hard to imagine such a forbidding, confident, strong man being chosen as a victim but perhaps his body had developed belatedly.

Besides, she knew children could be cruel. Her daughter, Eirwen, being slower than most, had suffered her share of jibes as a young girl. More often than she cared to remember, Carys had had to intervene to chase her tormentors away. Even now, most people didn't know how to handle her, even if they didn't mock her openly. So she could well believe the boys in James' village would have taken pleasure in taunting him for something he had no control over. There was safety in numbers, and one didn't have to be brave to assault a lonely boy when it was ten against one.

"I'm sorry," she murmured. "That must have been hard." Perhaps it had contributed to the forging of his stern personality. It would make sense if it had.

He nodded, his gaze still on the road ahead. "My parents were successful merchants, with ambitions of furthering their lot in life. One day, when my mother was nearing her fourth decade and their five children were no longer babes, they decided it was time to try and fulfil their dream. They went to a distant city on the continent called Venezia to trade with merchants from the Levant. Upon arrival, they met with silk traders from an even farther land called Egypt."

Now Carys thought she knew where he might be going with it. Presumably people from that mysterious land were possessed of black eyes, black eyes, and dark skin.

Just like he was.

"One of them, whose name my mother has always refused

to tell me, agreed to look after her and teach her all he knew about precious fabrics while my father went on to visit the neighboring islands in search of rare objects. Blown glass vases, mirrors and other luxury items they meant to take home. When they set left Venezia a month later, having been separated all this time, my mother was with child."

Though she had already guessed as much, Carys knew her shock would show on her face. Fortunately, James was still staring straight ahead.

"What did your father say?"

He shook his head slightly. "Even if he'd had doubts about who the father of this child was, it wouldn't have taken him long to see that the babe born nine months after my mother's sojourn in Venezia bore no resemblance to his other children but instead shared his coloring with their Egyptian host. It is not hard to imagine he would have felt the betrayal keenly, but I am proud to say he did not make me suffer for my mother's lapse."

Lapse... Had his mother gone to her lover willingly then, rather than been forced? She didn't dare ask. The confession was painful enough for James.

"What about the relationship between your parents?" she asked instead. Having to live with the proof of his wife's infidelity would have been hard for any man.

"I'm not sure what their relationship was before they left for Venezia but they managed to find a way to live together. What other choice did they have?" James asked bitterly. "I'm certain they would have preferred to go their separate ways but they had children to raise and a business to run. They just behaved as if nothing had happened. But I know they never left England again, and never made the fortune they'd hoped to make that summer."

"How terrible." Say what he might, James' father, or rather the man acting as his father, would have resented him not only for reminding him of his wife's betrayal, but also possibly for putting an end to his dreams of grandeur.

"Yes. When I was old enough to understand such matters, I started to wonder if my mother had been forced or seduced by the Egyptian merchant." Carys stayed silent. She had been wondering the same thing a moment ago. Did he have the answer to that terrible question? "Then one day, when I was about sixteen, she told me she had been unable to resist the lure of a man the likes of which she had never seen before. She told me I looked exactly like him and would one day be able to get all the women I wanted in my bed. It took me a long time to forgive her this confidence I didn't want to hear."

Yes, she could well imagine such a confession would have been a burden to him. But how not to sympathize with the woman? If the Egyptian merchant had possessed half of his son's dark appeal, it was no wonder she had succumbed to temptation. Hadn't Carys herself done the same that very afternoon?

Yes, she had. But, unlike James' mother at the time, she was not married. She had been free to act on the desire she felt toward James, and she shouldn't feel guilty about what they had done. She didn't exactly, or at least, she didn't feel she had betrayed her husband's memory. It was not so much the fact that they had shared intimacies only lovers shared that made her ill-at-ease, but rather the nature of those intimacies. Their tryst had been wild, and it had all been for her benefit.

James had not gotten any pleasure out of it, save the one of—

"Don't worry about it," he said in a low rumble.

Carys started. How had he guessed what she was thinking about? Had she talked out loud again, as she was wont to do? It was possible.

"And there is no shame in what we did," he continued. "It cannot have been new to you. I have not missed the way you speak about your late husband. You loved him and he loved you, so it stands to reason he would have wanted to ensure your satisfaction in bed. Do not tell me he didn't give you such intimate pleasure?"

Well, as far as personal questions went, this one was rather blunt. Why was she even surprised? The man was nothing if not blunt. Nevertheless, she answered.

"No, of course Dewi pleasured me, in more ways than one."

Carys blushed, unsure whether James would like her answer. Would he not prefer to hear he'd been the only one who'd ever made her explode in pleasure? Men had their ego, she knew, but she could not have lied and pretended Dewi had not cared about her needs or tried to bring her satisfaction in bed. He had. But he had never been that scandalous. He would never have lain with her outside in the open, at the risk of being walked upon. He had never made her beg for his attentions. He had never feasted on every part of her, including the most forbidden one. Up until that day, she would not have thought such a thing possible, and if she had, she would have thought James Mortimer the last man willing to indulge in such decadence.

"What about your wife? Did she give you pleasure?" she asked, not feeling equal to the task of discussing what she and Dewi had done or not done in bed. Being on horseback and not looking at one another helped with the awkwardness of the conversation, but it was still rather intimate.

"Yes, she did." He didn't hesitate. "I loved her, but, even if I hadn't, as I'm sure you're aware, it is much easier for a man to reach his pleasure anyway."

Another blunt statement. But he had a point, Carys had to admit. She had not felt much during her encounters with Alun, the first man she had taken to her bed after Dewi's death, but he certainly had, even if he had not felt anything special toward her. There definitely was an inequality between men and women's ability to feel pleasure, her discussions with her female friends had made that clear. Not many of them had a satisfactory marriage in that respect. As far as she could tell, she had been one of a few whose sensual needs had been fulfilled by their husbands.

Which only made what she had found with Dewi, and now with James, more special. She would fight for it.

"Why didn't you, then?"

"Didn't what?"

"Reach your pleasure, earlier. With m-me." Not having expected to have to spell it out, she was stammering dreadfully. Surely he knew what she meant? "Why didn't you take me after you..." Her voice trailed when he finally looked at her. His eyes were two black pools of fire.

"Because it is only too possible that, in taking you, I would lose a part of me. And I fear I haven't any left to spare."

It was a few days before Carys built up the courage to look James in the eye.

His unexpected, puzzling answer was lingering between them like heavy mist, muddling her thoughts, blurring her understanding. *In taking you, I would lose a part of me. And I haven't any left to spare.* What had he meant by those cryptic words?

She had no idea.

So she kept her distance as much as she could and, whenever they met, as was inevitable in such a small place, she did not exchange more than a perfunctory word with him. Mercifully, he did not push the issue, allowing her time to come to terms with the sudden and puzzling development in their relationship. The weather decided to help her by holding off rain and going as far as letting the sun shine. This clemency meant that she could spend her days away from the castle, foraging in the forest for plants to bring back to Avice.

Spring was now well underway and Carys let the simple pleasure of being out in nature wash over her. This was her first English spring, and it felt somehow significant, like a fresh opportunity to be seized.

But a fresh opportunity to do what?

All she could think of revolved around James. But he didn't seem prepared to give them a chance, crippled by fears she didn't understand.

In taking you, I would lose a part of me. And I haven't any left to spare.

Just *what* did he mean? It was an odd thing to say, as anyone would agree. But perhaps the oddest thing of all was the thought whirring in her own head in response to his statement: *In allowing you to take me, I would gain a part of me I refused to accept I needed. And it would finally make me complete.*

Really, what nonsense this all was. She had better focus on tonight's dinner. The ground was carpeted in soft dandelion leaves waiting for her, all the way from where she was standing to the oaks she could see spreading their branches in the distance. They, rather than James Mortimer, would benefit from her attention that afternoon.

Later, with her basket full, she decided to go to the herb garden to see if she could find something to add to the leaves she'd gathered. Encouraged by the generous sunshine, the first shoots were coming out. Perhaps some burnet, borage or chives would have dared venture above the soil. But in the end, Carys didn't make it past the stone arch doorway. Matthew and Branwen were standing by the bench in the far corner and something about their attitude told her an interruption would not be welcome. Their fingers were entwined and they were gazing into one another's eyes. There was such raw emotion on their faces that she could not help a smile. Was there anything better than to love and be loved in return?

If there was, she'd yet to find out what it might be.

Slowly, so as not to alert them to her presence, Carys retreated back into the lists. But before she could turn around and disappear, Matthew did something that froze her into place. He fell to his knees in front of Branwen and kissed her stomach. There was such reverence in the gesture that there was no need to hear what her daughter had just told him. She was with child at last. As if to confirm it, Branwen started crying. Even from a distance, it was clear that these were happy tears. And unless Carys was mistaken, Matthew was sobbing as well, holding his wife as tightly as if he wanted them to fuse as one.

In a way, they had, in the form of a babe they would soon get to hold in their arms.

Her first grandchild.

Carys found her own cheeks were wet with tears when she took a final step back to hide herself from view. A grandchild. How wonderful. She had started to suspect Branwen's secret but had not dared to hope, or talk to her about it in case she was mistaken. Now she knew it wouldn't be long before they had another discussion.

"Are you all right?"

The deep voice sent a shiver up her whole body. Hastily she wiped the tears from her cheeks before turning to look at James. He would know she'd been crying but there was no helping it. If he hadn't suspected it already, he would not have asked the question.

"Yes, yes. I'm... I'll be fine."

"Is it my fault?" he asked, looking more anxious than she had ever seen him. His usually inscrutable face now appeared ridden with guilt. "Was I too forceful with you the other day? Is that why you've been avoiding me these last few days?"

Forceful? That wasn't the word she would have used. Outrageous? Most definitely. Did she regret it? No. Did she want more?

A hundred times yes.

"No. You did nothing wrong and I was not crying because of any distress you might have caused me," she assured him, realizing only now that by having avoided him, she had allowed him to worry about his treatment of her the day on the beach. It had not been her intention.

"What then? There is something."

Her eyes burned anew with unshed tears. Yes, there *was* something. "Unless I am mistaken, I am soon to have a grandchild."

James' whole body seemed to relax now that she'd made clear he was not responsible for her bout of crying. Slowly, so as to reassure him further, she nudged him toward the arch doorway and nodded at Matthew and Branwen, who were still locked in a tender embrace.

"That's wonderful news," he said, sounding somewhat gruffer than usual.

Carys stilled. Was he fighting tears as well? A smile came to tease her lips. It certainly sounded as if the impassible man was moved at the idea of a woman being with child. Who would have thought it? Every day she discovered a little bit more about him. He could be passionate, whimsical, protective, emotional even, in his own way. And every day she liked him a bit more. Moved herself, she took her hand in his. Just like that, the awkwardness she had felt in the last few days was gone. She just wanted to share this incredible moment with him because she knew why the news had affected him so much. Having lost his children, he would have thought never to know the joy of becoming a grandfather.

For different reasons, they had both been in the same situation. And now, they were both to know a joy they had thought out of their reach.

"You know, this baby is going to be my grandchild without actually being related to me by blood," she murmured. He knew now she had not given birth to Branwen or Eirwen. "By the same token, it will be yours as well. Didn't you tell me you and Matthew had more of a father-to-son relationship than anything else? That you helped raise him when he was adopted by the late Lord Sheridan as a young boy?"

He hesitated. "Aye, I did, when he had no one else to look up to. But we always knew I was not really his father. Richard is, and now they have been reunited."

Though he didn't say the rest, she understood all too well.
Now he doesn't need me anymore.

Her heart melted. Raised by a man who had not been his real father, taking care of a boy who was not of his loins, he'd never felt secure in his place. Except as Joanne's husband. But his wife was now dead, and he did not have anything to show for their years of love. His children were long gone, as was she, and he didn't have anyone left.

It was a lonely life, even more lonely than hers, who at least had Branwen and Eirwen to love.

"It makes no difference whether Matthew has been reunited with Richard or not. You were the one who was there for him when he needed it the most. He will not forget it just because he is a grown man and about to have a child of his own. On the contrary, he will want you to be a part of his son or daughter's life." Certain of herself, she gave his hand a squeeze. "In any case, I hear it was thanks to you that son and father were reunited. He will be grateful for that, if for nothing else."

She had heard the whole story through Branwen during their travel to England.

A year ago, the carpenter had come to Sheridan Manor in search of Matthew's mother, Rose. He'd just lost his wife and now that he was free, it had been his intention to marry the love of his life at last. Unfortunately, the poor maid had been long dead by then. Up until that day Matthew had believed his father to be an unscrupulous nobleman who had raped his mother and never bothered to find out if the encounter had resulted in a child.

Overwhelmed, unable to tell the devastated man the truth, Matthew had let Richard go without revealing he had fathered a son during his week of happiness with Rose some thirty years ago.

James, alerted by instinct, had suspected Matthew would come to regret his cowardice and want to know where to find his true father when he finally found the courage to speak to him. He'd befriended Richard and taken it upon himself to ask where he was residing. And indeed, less than a month later, the information had come in useful. Connor had summoned the carpenter all the way to Esgyrn Castle in Wales.

Thanks to James, father and son had been able not only to meet, but also to start to build a relationship. Without him, they might not have found each other again, and Richard would not now be living at Sheridan Manor. Matthew, who was a good man, would not forget what he owed the steward, just because his wife was about to give birth. On the contrary, becoming a father would show him all he owed to the man who had raised him as his.

"You have nothing to fear," she concluded. "This babe will be your grandchild as much as he will be mine."

James swallowed. Carys' words of reassurance meant everything to him but just as important was the fact that she had seemed to get over her new shyness in front of him. For days she'd gone out of her way to avoid being alone with him and he'd hated it.

But she had just taken him by the hand and was smiling the radiant smile that never failed to clutch at his heart. Relief almost floored him. He had so dreaded to see her withdraw from him after their encounter on the beach. It would have been his fault if she had, and it would have been well deserved. Lost to his desire for her, he had been rather scandalous. At the time he'd had the impression that she had loved everything he'd done but the fact remained. He had taken liberties he should not have taken, and allowed his desire to overwhelm him. Never had he tasted a woman in such a scandalous manner before, but it had been unstoppable, delicious. He'd wanted to devour her whole, make her his in every way he could.

He still did.

The urge was more than a little frightening, because only last month he had thought to be done with women. When Margaret had tried, not so subtly, to make him understand she would be amenable to an arrangement between them, he had balked at the idea. He was too settled in his ways for the headache this would create, too old to even want to attempt something of the sort, too wary of the pain it could bring. Hope and lust were all well and good when you were a young lad eager to start a family, but a man his age should know better and be able to be satisfied with a more sensible arrangement. There was always an accommodating woman or two to be found in the village when his body demanded release and surely that was all he needed?

At least that was what he'd thought for years.

Now he was wondering if the issue had not been with the women offering to give him a second chance. None had captured his interest, they had only stirred his senses long enough for him to ease the tension in his body. But now... What had seemed unthinkable with Margaret didn't frighten him half as much with Carys. Perhaps with a woman like her, he could find both pleasure in bed *and* contentment outside of it.

Yes. Perhaps. On principle.

Because in actual fact, he knew it would never happen. He was still too scared, and he didn't see how that would change.

Years later he still remembered the awful, gut-wrenching pain of being handed a stillborn baby, or worse, of holding the dead body of a child you had rocked to sleep, learned to love and hoped to see grow one day into a man. Nothing would convince him to risk such a thing again.

No.

It was best to carry on like he had for years—and forget all about his unfortunate desire for delightful Welsh women.

Chapter Six

"A letter from Esgyrn Castle, my lord."

The rider bowed to the people assembled around the table before handing the missive to Matthew, who smiled his thanks and instructed him to go to the kitchen for some food and ale. The dusty man went gratefully.

"This will be news of Esyllt and the babe. I expect she will be safely delivered by now. This second baby followed his sister Gwenllian rather quickly, but I don't think anyone was surprised, given how devoted to one another my brother and his wife are." He threw a quick glance at the letter and let out a burst of laughter. "Well, it appears my dear sister-in-law has given birth to a boy this time, if you would believe it! Little Rhys. My brother finally has a son. Miracles do happen, or it would seem."

James smiled to himself. He had thought exactly the same thing a year ago, when he'd received news that Matthew, whom everyone here had thought would remain unmarried, had found himself a wife. Would there be a third miracle at Sheridan Manor? One that involved him for a change?

Just then, his gaze met Carys'. She flushed. His body surged.

She averted her eyes. His heart leapt. Yes, perhaps there would be. Miracles came in all shapes and sizes, and the best ones came under the guise of women who brought color and excitement to men's lives. Connor, then Matthew, and now him. Were all the men at Sheridan Manor destined to fall for Welsh women?

Was he falling of her?

No, surely what he felt wasn't that deep?

"I am so glad for Esyllt. I must write to congratulate her, and tell her my own happy news," Branwen said, placing a hand on her still flat stomach.

She had announced earlier that morning that she was expecting her husband's first child. Both James and Carys had feigned ignorance of the fact, not wanting to spoil the moment for the parents-to-be. He had enjoyed sharing a secret with her. While Richard had enthused about the birth to come, the two of them had exchanged a glance full of complicity. Dear God, he was really getting old, if such looks were enough to make his heart flutter. As a young man, he would have preferred to exchange lusty looks hinting at a night of debauchery. But this had felt just as satisfying.

Once everyone had offered their congratulations, Matthew had looked at both him and Richard and declared that his son was to have the best two grandfathers he could have hoped for. James' heart had almost burst with joy. Carys had been right the previous day. They would all be one big family here at Sheridan Manor.

Perhaps against all odds he would not end his life alone.

"Do you know, our babies will be cousins," Branwen carried on. "Who would have thought it? Oh, I'm so happy."

Carys smiled at her daughter. James knew what she would be thinking. Branwen had been happy since her wedding to Matthew, but she was now positively glowing.

"So am I." Matthew took his wife's hand and lifted it to his mouth. "You will allow me to add a note to your missive, Raven, so I can ask Esyllt to be godmother to our child. I promised her on the day of Gwenllian's christening that she would be my first child's godmother. I will be only too glad to honor my promise now that the time has come. Unless you object?"

A giggle. "Of course not. I want no other than her and Eirwen. And, of course, Connor will be the godfather."

"Of course."

"Let us drink to little Rhys' health!" Richard declared, raising his cup in the air. "May he be blessed with many more cousins in the years to come."

Branwen blushed and hid her face in the crook of her husband's neck. At first James could not identify the odd sensation bubbling in his chest. Then he realized that it was anticipation. For the first time in years, he had something to look forward to.

His gaze once again landed on Carys.

Yes. Perhaps his life was not quite over yet.

The rest of the meal was spent in a jovial atmosphere. Once everyone had washed their hands in the bowls of scented water, James drew Carys to one side.

"Can I have a word with you?" he asked in a breath, careful not to be overheard

She nodded and waited until they were alone to turn to him, eyes aglow. "What is it?"

It was only then he realized he had no idea why he had asked her to stay behind. What did he want to tell her? He didn't know. So he just kissed her.

It was a gentle kiss, emotional, but intense nonetheless. Or perhaps it was precisely *because* it was driven by something other than lust that it was so intense. They worshipped one another's mouth, knowing they didn't have anything to prove.

Their tongues swirled in a sensual dance rather than spar in a frenzied exchange. They took their time, savoring rather than devouring each other.

And his whole body surged in response.

His soul vibrated.

This was more than a kiss, it was the beginning of something. When they finally drew away, Carys stared at him a long moment, a dazed look in her eyes.

"What did you do that for?"

Another excellent question. Another one he did not have the answer to. But something about the announcement they had just heard had made it impossible for him not to kiss her. Anticipation was coursing up and down his spine and for the first time since Joanne's death, he wanted to recapture a bit of spontaneity, a bit of the insouciance he and his wife had shared. He had become so dour since then, so stuck in his ways. He'd wanted to act, and not worry about the consequences for once.

"I didn't kiss you the other day on the beach," he murmured against her lips. "And it was eating at me. I thought it was time I rectified the mistake."

"Oh, but you most definitely kissed me," Carys whispered back, bringing her lips to his ear. "Only... not on the lips."

Everything within James tightened. Jesus, was the woman trying to make him mad with lust by alluding to what he had done? If so, she was going the right way about it. He had not been able to forget what had happened on that blanket. His delight at seeing that her shift was indeed embroidered with flowers all along the hem, the joy bubbling in his veins at the thought of finally being able to taste her, her moans of ecstasy when she had spasmed around his fingers, and the satisfaction of knowing he had rendered her boneless, everything was etched into his mind for eterntity.

"I still don't know why you didn't take me afterward," she

carried on, her voice low and seductive. "Your explanation was interrupted by the arrival of the women and children and then later while we rode back home, I will admit I didn't understand what you told—"

Her voice trailed when he drew away from her, all desire doused.

Running a hand through his hair, he started to pace around the room. He'd not taken her because he could not, and now he would have to tell her why. At the time, he'd been relieved his explanation had been cut short but things had become too personal between them; he could not let her worry she had done something wrong or think that he didn't want her. He knew his statement about not having any spare parts of himself to lose would have puzzled her. But how to explain his reticence to bed her?

Better to start at the beginning.

"I told you that day I didn't have any children. Well, I did, once. My wife gave birth to four babies, and I buried them all." His chest tightened at the memory, as he'd expected, but now that he had started, he found that he did not want to stop. "My two daughters, conceived first, were both born dead. The first one came out before her time, and there was nothing we could do. The other, we were told, had been strangled by the umbilical cord during the long and difficult labor. Again, there was nothing to be done but to accept the loss. Joanne was heartbroken, and blamed herself for not being able to deliver her swiftly enough. I was devastated also but had to find the strength to be there for her, convince her she had done nothing wrong."

Carys was frozen in horror by the revelation. The pain of losing one child after another was hard to imagine. She waited, because he had mentioned four children, and only told her what had happened to his two poor daughters. Where were his sons?

"After those traumatic experiences it took me a while to

agree to Joanne's entreaties that I give her another child." He shook his head as if fearing she would judge him for refusing his wife her dearest wish. She did not judge him. No one could know how they would react after going through such tragedy. She might have done the same in his place. "I gave her pleasure, of course, and we even made love on occasion, but I always made sure not to reach my release inside her. I could not bear to lose another child, or her, in childbed. The two births had been hard on her. I did not see how a third one would not end in tragedy."

"Of course." It was all too understandable.

"Then one day, despite my carefulness, she announced she was with child again. I was petrified, but did my best to hide my feelings from her, not wanting to spoil her joy or worry her unduly. Six months later she gave birth to the most beautiful babe I had ever seen. We were happy again, and my fears receded to the back of my mind. Two years after Edward's birth, she told me we were to have another child. Anthony was born on Christmas Day, the exact copy of his brother. For a while, everything was perfect."

For a while. Yes. Until disaster struck again. Carys braced herself.

"What happened to them?"

Did she want to know? Yes. If James could find the courage to speak out, she could certainly listen.

"For Anthony, we don't know. Four months after his birth, we found him one morning, dead in his cot. No one could give us any explanation as to what that might be. I still don't understand what could have happened. We were told that it was God's will, and that we weren't the first or the last parents to experience such loss. A meagre consolation, as I'm sure you'll agree." He rubbed a shaky hand over his face. Carys could barely breathe. Years later, his pain was still so vivid that she could feel the echoes of it rippling through her. She could not begin to imagine what he had gone through. "He was such a happy, lively little boy. When I found him, cold and still, I could not accept it. I held him all day and—"

He stopped and clenched his fists. Carys stayed silent, because there was nothing to say. It was horrid, and nothing she could have said would change that.

She had heard about these mysterious, sudden deaths. One summer, two women in her village had lost their babes that way in the space of a week. Her neighbor had been a friend, so, naturally, Carys had gone to offer her condolences. Lost to her grief, unable to make sense of the tragedy that had hit her, desperate to find a culprit, the woman had rounded on her.

"You're lucky to be unable to bear children!" she'd spat. "At least you'll never know the pain of losing a babe."

Yes, she was a lucky woman indeed, who would never know the joy of holding her babe in her arms.

She'd not responded.

Pushing the memories away, she took James' hand in hers. "What about Edward?" Though this was painful, she didn't want to give him the impression she didn't care about his second son's death. Each of the boys deserved to be talked about, because they had each been equally loved.

"About a year after Anthony's death, Edward came back home one evening, complaining of cramps in his stomach. We asked him what he'd been doing that day and were told he'd drank some of the stagnant water by the marshes." James' eyes were void of emotion, his voice flat but this time Carys didn't make the mistake of thinking him impassible. He was anything but. "He suffered for days. Just like with the others, there was nothing I could do, but this time it was even worse. I had to watch all the while, knowing I could not help, until he died."

"Oh, James."

Lord, this was unbearable.

"After that I found it impossible to make love to my wife in the normal way. I just couldn't bear to father another child, only to lose him in turn. She understood, I think, and never complained, never blamed me. But it meant we could never quite recapture what we'd had at the start of our marriage. On her death bed I told her I wish I could have acted differently, but of course it was too late. She died without having joined with me, her husband, properly, for years."

Carys squeezed the hand she was still holding. *"Mae'n ddrwg gen i."*

Telling him she was sorry, and in Welsh, would not help in any way. But she needed to say it nonetheless. Why had she asked him anything? They had kissed, it had been wonderful, and instead of basking in the moment she'd gone and ruined it all with her stupid question, reminding him of his losses, his pain and his regrets. Couldn't she have let it be?

"So in answer to your question, I didn't take you that day on the beach because I could not. I cannot risk losing control. It's been years since I have been able to—"

To let himself go in a woman's arms.

He didn't need to finish the sentence. She'd understood what he'd not been able to say. But she knew with her there was no risk, as she would never conceive. Should she tell him as much? Was she brave enough? Was it the right time? They were talking about him right now.

"I'm sorry. I shouldn't have kissed you, or touched you in the way I did, because I'm never going to give you what you want. I cannot."

Something fell to the bottom of Carys' stomach. He thought she only wanted him for the pleasure his body could give her when he possessed her. He thought she was looking for a lover.

She did not. She was not. What was between them was more than that.

Before she could say anything, he left.

"Carys, there you are. I looked for you everywhere yesterday and could not find you."

Carys smiled at Richard. "No, you couldn't have. I went to the village in the afternoon with Eirwen."

The two of them had gone to Mistress Ivy to tell her about Branwen being with child, knowing she would be delighted at the news. She had been.

"I knew there wasn't any problem with your daughter," she said, abandoning the pots and plants she'd been sorting out to take her hands in hers. "Now that she has seen for herself that she can do it, she will have the beautiful family she craves. Sometimes it's all in the mind."

"Yes."

And sometimes it was not, Carys couldn't help but think. Sometimes there really was something broken in a woman's body. Mistress Ivy must have seen the pain slashing through her guts because her smile wavered.

"I'm sorry. That was not the best thing for me to—"

She cut her with a swift smile. "You couldn't have known. And you're right. Now that Branwen has seen there is nothing wrong with her, she will be able to relax and give her husband the family they both want."

Carys certainly hoped so. With her conversation with James still preying on her mind, she could not help a sense of foreboding. All her life she had focused on getting with child. That, for her, had been the difficult part. She had not stopped to think beyond the conception, or even imagined that there could be problems afterward. But, oh, now she knew just how many there could be. The story she'd heard that morning would haunt her for months to come. James and Joanne had suffered so much! Please let Branwen and Matthew not go through what they had gone through. She wasn't sure how any of the people at Sheridan Manor would bear it.

"I just brewed some lemon balm tea," Mistress Ivy said, an obvious attempt at distraction. "Would you like a cup?"

"With pleasure."

While they talked and drank the fragrant tea sweetened with honey, Eirwen hovered by the table where dozens of plants had been piled up, ready to be sorted before being dried. By the time the tea had been drunk and they were ready to go, the table looked very different.

Instead of taking exception to Eirwen's meddling, as some people might have, the healer arched a brow. "Does your daughter know about plants?" she asked, surveying the arrangement. "She's not only made neat piles and gotten rid of the less than perfect leaves, but she's organized them according to the properties they possess. Look, here are the ones used for stomach complaints, there are the ones that can combat fever, and so on. I cannot believe she placed them thus at random."

Carys frowned. *Was* Eirwen knowledgeable about plants? She'd certainly never hinted at an interest in healing. Intrigued herself, she translated the question. Her daughter reddened and nodded, as if admitting to a guilty secret.

"Apparently, she does," Carys told the healer, amazed and proud all at once.

"She must do, because she's done exactly what I would have done, and even started to remove the leaves from the stalks in preparation for drying. This is most helpful."

After that, the woman had asked them to come back another day to see if Eirwen was as knowledgeable about plants as she suspected she was. As it happened, with the growing population in the village, she had been hoping to get some help. Carys had been only too glad to agree. It would be wonderful if, thanks to her unsuspected skill, her daughter could make a difference in the community and get to know people. Her knowledge of English would also improve that way. At the moment, she was barely able to communicate with people other than her and Branwen. Mistress Ivy did not seem concerned, however, when Carys pointed the potential problem out.

"We'll find a way to understand one another. It seems to me she doesn't need much guidance anyway," she's added, nodding toward the table. "She knows what she's doing."

"Then, of course we'll come back."

Eirwen, when consulted, nodded enthusiastically.

Carys had left the hut feeling ten times lighter. This was just what Eirwen needed, a new friend, a way to fit in her new environment. It seemed both her daughters would find their happily ever after in England. Who would have thought? Blessed be Matthew Hunter, who was responsible for this turn of events.

Heat invaded her, because it was not only Branwen and Eirwen's life he had changed. He was also responsible for her meeting with James. And the steward might potentially be *her* happily ever after.

"Did you need anything?" she asked Richard, who was still waiting, an expectant look on his face.

Before he could answer, she reached out for her embroidery basket. An idea had just popped into her head. She would decorate a blanket with ivy leaves to thank the kind healer for her offer to tutor Eirwen, and she wanted to start immediately. As it happened, she had just purchased new threads and so had the perfect colors for what she wanted to do, different hues of green.

"Yes, a word with you, if I may." Richard walked over to her.

Carys stilled. There seemed to be a new intensity about him today, one that unsettled her. "You know, I'm so glad we're able to understand each other at last."

Her heart started to flutter in her chest. They had been able to understand one another for months. Why was he coming to her now?

"Are you?" she croaked, placing the embroidery basket back in its place. It was obvious she wouldn't be making any blankets right now. Her discussion with Richard would require all her powers of concentration.

"Yes. And I think you might know why."

Yes, unfortunately, she thought she might know why. She had not missed the looks he'd thrown her as they had traveled from Wales to England together. He had been smitten with her. But just like it had been with James, they had been prevented from getting to know one another by the language barrier. She had thought he might come to speak about his feelings for her as soon as she was able to communicate in English. Then, when months had passed and he had kept silent, she had allowed herself to relax and hope she had been mistaken. Perhaps not being able to understand him had made her imagine things, or he had found someone else who piqued his interest here at Sheridan Manor and forgotten about her.

Well, evidently, she'd not been mistaken and he'd only been biding his time, becoming her friend. It was clear that he was about to open his heart to her. Her own heart sank in her chest because, although she thought him perfectly amiable, her feelings for him would never be more than friendship and she hated the idea of causing him pain.

Thinking it preferable to stop him before he could open up, she started. "Richard, forgive me, but I—"

"Please, let me speak first," he cut in, coming a step closer. "Yesterday, when my son and his wife announced they were to have a child, I realized that a new chapter was opening in my life, one that would be different from the one I lived as a young man. Seeing Branwen becoming a mother will have made you think the same, I think."

Carys could only nod. It was true that hearing the announcement had made her feel life had suddenly changed pace. And she *had* started to ask herself questions about what she wanted. But none of the answers had involved Richard.

Hearing no protest, he pushed on. "You and I are of an age and like each other. We already live in the same place. I think we could find a way of ending our days together."

At any time, Carys would have found it hard to hear such a declaration. With the memory of the kiss she and James had shared the day before, it was excruciating. For a moment she had hoped to have a future with *him*. But then she'd ruined it all by reminding him of his losses and forcing him to explain why he would never consider being with a woman again.

Still, perhaps the damage was not irreparable. Perhaps she could make him see that she was someone with whom he need not fear anything. She would have to find a way to convince him, bare her own pain if necessary. For now, though, she had a more pressing problem to deal with.

Richard.

She looked at him, utterly at a loss. How could she respond to his offer without letting her dismay show? Because she was about to refuse, of that she had no doubt. It was not only the fact that she had no real feelings for him that guided her decision. The nature of his offer grated. He sounded as if she had no other option but to accept him on pain of ending up all alone and unhappy, he seemed to suggest that no one else would want her, he made her feel like a woman past her best, with little left to hope for before death finally claimed her.

If he wanted to woo her, he was going about it the wrong way.

Really, the contrast between the two men was shocking. Richard had not even touched her while he talked of a future together, James had not promised her anything but he had kissed her as if his life depended on it. Richard was appealing to her reason, seeing her as a companion with whom to share his old age, James had attacked her senses, treated her like a woman still at the height of her beauty, and made her body explode in pleasure.

She took a step backward and felt the wall against her shoulders, blocking her retreat. The lord have mercy on her. How would she get out of this without hurting Richard's feelings? He was not a bad man, but he was not the man for her, she had never been more certain of anything.

"I thank you for the offer but I'm not sure we would be suited to—"

"You haven't allowed me to try to persuade you, that's why." He caught up with her and, wrapping an arm about her waist, drew her to him. "I think you should allow me to show you how it would be between us before you say anything."

And he did just that. He showed her exactly how she imagined things would be between them. Reasonable. Unexciting. Dull. His kiss was gentle, and perfectly pleasant, but all Carys could think was that this man would never do anything to shock or even surprise her. He would not expose her to his gaze before pleasuring her, he would not lick her as if he could not get enough of what her body had to offer, he would not compliment her on her taste afterward.

Did she want such a companion? The answer was clear in her mind. She did not, not when a man like James Mortimer was available. She shook her head. No, it was not even that. Even if she hadn't spent a scandalous afternoon with him the other day, even if they had not shared a fiery kiss the previous morning, she would not have been tempted by a life with Richard, who could only ever be a friend. With Dewi she'd had love and passion, she could not settle for anything less now, when nothing obliged her to even be with someone. Why shackle herself to someone who would never make her heart flutter or her body hum in desire?

She drew back as gently as she could, and he let her go. Which only proved she was right to think they would never suit. If he was not even prepared to fight to keep her in his arms, he would never do anything to give her the impression she was the center of his life.

"Richard. Please. This is not a good idea, and you know it." Would that he realized it himself! Surely he'd felt how passionless their kiss had been?

"You haven't even had time to think about—"

He stopped mid-sentence and his gaze flickered to a place to her left. Carys turned to see what had caught his attention and her heart dropped to her knees.

James was standing in the door frame, the expression on his face dark as thunder.

"I think Carys has made her wishes clear, wouldn't you say?" he growled. "She doesn't want you. Let her go."

That wasn't exactly what she had said, but now was not the time to point it out. Because it was the truth anyway.

She hastened to the door, sensing the men were about to lash out at each other. Fleeing was the coward way out, but she couldn't bear to be the reason for the two friends' disagreement.

"I'm sorry. Please don't fight on my account, it's n-not worth it," she stammered, before running away.

Once he and Richard were alone, James planted himself in front of the carpenter. Tension sizzled, filling the whole room, but neither of them moved. They were almost of a height, and both boasted athletic physiques. Because of it, the outcome of a fight between them was hard to predict. Still, James sensed he would emerge the victor, because of what was at stake.

Carys.

"If we were twenty or thirty years younger I believe you would have planted your fist in my face by now," Richard said after a while.

James knew he most likely looked about to do just that, even if he was doing his best to suppress the urge. When he had walked into the great hall and seen Carys and his friend locked in an intimate embrace, his stomach had flipped in his chest at what he'd thought was a betrayal. Only the morning before, he had kissed her, and confided his deepest, most painful secret, surely she could have waited more than a day before throwing herself into another man's arms?

Then once the red mist had dissipated, he'd noticed how her arms were limp by her sides, how she appeared stunned rather than lost to desire and he'd understood that not only had she not initiated the kiss, but she was not stirred by it. There was no lust in her, or even interest. By the time she had angled her body away from Richard and told him it was not a good idea, James had understood that she did not want him.

This was a misunderstanding, nothing more. He had no reason to be mad at Carys, or to rip Richard to pieces. And so he would do neither, as tempting as it might be.

He walked over to the window and looked into the distance in a bid to master his temper. With luck, the peaceful view at his feet would help restore some calm into him. It took a while but when he felt himself again and able to talk to his friend, he turned to face him.

"The fact that I didn't hit you has nothing to do with our age." James ran a hand through his hair. "I would like nothing more than to ensure your mouth is too mangled to allow you to impose your kisses on Carys from now on. But unfortunately for me, I think your intentions toward her are honorable."

If the carpenter had been too forceful, or thought to take advantage of Carys in any way, he would have made him regret his actions, but it had been nothing like that. The kiss had been too tame, too respectable to be threatening in any way. If Richard had only been after a meaningless night in her arms, James might have taken exception to it but he could tell that wasn't the case. The offer had been for far more.

"Of course my intentions are honorable," Richard huffed. "Who do you take me for? I want to offer her a second chance at life. Carys is a remarkable woman, and has been alone for far too long. She deserves to be happy."

"Yes," James said through gritted teeth. This, at least, they could agree on. She *was* a remarkable woman, and she did deserve happiness.

"Alas, she's not interested in what I have to offer. 'Tis clear she has her mind set on another man."

James' heart skipped a beat. She did? Bloody hell. He'd only just discovered Richard was a contender in Carys' affection, and now he was told someone else was lurking in the shadows? Would he have to have words with all the men at Sheridan Manor? Or was this mysterious suitor residing in the village?

"Who?" he growled, already knowing he would throttle the man if he dared toy with her. The blacksmith? The baker? Not Luke's new farm hand, surely?

Richard threw him a look he could only have described as incredulous. "Are you really that blind? You, of course."

A riot of emotions assaulted James all at once, causing him to stare at his friend. Incredulity, pride, anger, joy, possessiveness, fear. In the end, anger won. It was easier that way, safer.

"You mean you offered to make her your..." He stopped, not knowing what word to use exactly. Was Richard ready to marry

her or had he merely proposed a mutually beneficial arrangement? He didn't know. "You kissed her, all the while thinking
she wanted to be with me?"

He planted himself in front of his friend, just like he had
earlier. Though this time it would be clear he would pounce at
the least provocation, Richard pushed at his chest, not in the
least impressed.

"Yes, I did, because, you big lout, she might want you, but
you do not want *her*, do you? Or at least not enough to offer her
the second chance you agreed so readily that she deserves. And
why? Because you're too much of a coward to admit to what you
feel for her!" There was another push. But James was too
stunned to retaliate. "So what do you want? For her to spend the
rest of her life alone, at the mercy of passing men who think
they can amuse themselves with her? To be unloved and unpro-
tected? Don't tell me you're such a selfish bastard!"

"I..."

What could he say? He wasn't sure. Did he want Carys?
Yes. Was he a coward? Probably, because he refused to admit
his feelings to her, and even to himself. Was he selfish? Definitely, since the idea of her belonging to another man, or even
going to his bed for a harmless dalliance, ripped at his guts
despite the sorry truth that he had not promised her anything.
He could not be with her, and yet he didn't want her to be with
anyone else.

It was madness.

Only the day before he had confided in her about the pain
of his losses, hoping she would understand why he could not be
with her, or at least why he needed time to accept this new
development. And before he'd had time to even try, he'd been
forced by Richard's actions to take a stand, and make a decision.

James had never liked being cornered and he liked it even
less now, when it was crucial he did not make any mistakes.

"Let it be. This is none of your concern." He wanted nothing more than to put an end to this painful conversation. Why had he felt the need to interrupt the confrontation? Carys had never been in any danger. She had made her wishes clear and the carpenter would never have pushed her beyond what she was comfortable with. His intervention hadn't been needed.

"No. Unfortunately, Carys has made it clear that what happened to her wasn't my concern. And so it seems that I, too, am destined to spend the rest of my life alone."

Richard sounded so bitter that the remainder of James' anger faded away.

He sighed, knowing his friend was more than owed another chance at happiness himself, having lost the love of his life without having had the opportunity of living with her. James' wife had died too early and he had endured his share of trials but he had at least had a number of blissful years with Joanne. Richard had only spent one week with Rose, Matthew's mother, before fate had wrenched them apart.

But perhaps all was not lost.

"My friend, it would seem I am not the only blind one around here," he said slowly. As long as they were talking about someone else's inadequacies, he had no problem carrying on the discussion.

"What does that mean?"

It was James' turn to look incredulous. "You do not have to spend the rest of your life alone if you don't want to. Or have you not seen the way Avice looks at you?"

"Avice? The cook?"

"Do you know any other? She's been fawning after you since the day you arrived." Richard was still blinking, stunned by what was evidently news for him, but James knew he was not mistaken. He had known the cook for years and the infatuation was obvious to him. The woman was smitten. "I was wondering why you'd grown so fat. 'Twill be all the tarts she makes for you, I'm thinking. The rest of us are not so lucky. Not that the food is bad, of course, she's the best cook we've ever had at Sheridan Manor. I particularly like her pigeon pies. I have no idea what she puts in them but I have never tasted better ones. Sage perhaps? Or sweet onions?"

He was blabbering on because he could see that Richard had been struck by his revelation and he wanted to give him time to recover. After a while, he did.

"Avice?" The carpenter still sounded dazed but not displeased. On the contrary. "Do you think so?"

"I don't think so, I know so." James slapped him on the shoulder. Really, how had the man not seen anything? "And now that I've told you, you will see it also."

"Well, it would seem that we are a sad pair of idiots, because neither of us can see what is staring at us in the face."

"Yes. It would seem we are."

Because now he'd heard Richard's assertion that Carys was interested in him, everything made sense. It was the only way to explain her reaction to his kiss, the only reason she would have admitted out loud to being unable to forget what they had done on the beach. Even more to the point, he guessed she had only allowed him to touch her in that manner because of the attraction she felt. She would have pushed him away otherwise, like she had Richard.

Something would have to change, now that his eyes had been opened.

He would have to stop being a sad idiot and be a man once more.

Chapter Seven

"James!"

Carys gasped when she turned to her side, only to find herself face to face with the man she'd been thinking about all evening. For once he was not wearing a black tunic. In fact, he was not wearing anything. Not even a shift. Her whole body dissolved at the sight of his chest. Heavens. She had guessed he would be lean and chiseled but this...

"W-what are you doing here? It's my bed."

"I know. That is precisely why I'm here."

A hand closed over her breast and squeezed. The feel of his warm, slightly callused palm on her skin was incredible. Her *skin*... Another gasp escaped her lips when she realized she shouldn't be able to feel him thus. Where had her shift gone? Why was she naked? She never slept naked. An arm snaked around her waist, drawing her close to a furry chest before she could find an explanation for this unusual occurrence.

"You shouldn't—"

"Hush, let me do this, sweet. I'm dying with the need to taste you again and I know it's what you want too."

Oh, yes, she did want this. She wanted this, and more, but

something was odd, and she could not place her finger on it. Then she understood. They were talking in Welsh together. When had James learned to speak her language so well? And why was she worrying about something like this when he was spreading her legs to give him access to her most secret opening?

A tongue licked the cream that had pooled between her thighs and she stopped thinking. Let him speak in the language of his Egyptian ancestors if he wanted, as long as he gave her the release she was already desperate for.

"So good," he growled, swirling his tongue around the soft folds waiting for him. "Let me lick you like I did at the beach. And then I'll give you what you really want. What I haven't given anyone in years. You won't even have to beg this time."

"Yes!" He had vanquished his fears, and decided he could be with her. He was finally going to take her. Heat blazed through her at the thought.

"James!"

Carys woke up with her heart pounding, her breathing ragged and her hand between her legs. A finger was poised at her entrance, ready to plunge in. She was alone.

A dream.

That was all it had been. James was not really in her bed, had not really been speaking to her in Welsh, had not really been licking at her intimate flesh.

She stayed very still, her blood drumming a fierce rhythm in her ears. It was not the first time she had dreamed about what they had done on the beach, admittedly, but it was the first time it had sent her into such a frenzy, as well as the first time she had touched herself while she dreamed. Thank God she was not sleeping with Eirwen anymore, or she would have died of mortification. Her daughter, who had become friends with Avice's niece, had asked to sleep in her chamber a few weeks ago. Carys had been only too happy to allow her to. Now, more than ever, she was glad she'd done so.

Because it meant she could finish what the dream had started.

Almost of its own accord, her finger glided over the seam of her sex. She was swollen, throbbing and wet, thanks to what the wicked, naked man had been doing in her dream. She was so ready she knew she would explode in no time. Since Dewi's death, in the absence of a real lover with whom to indulge her senses, she'd had no choice but to give herself pleasure and had become quite adept at it.

But usually, it was her late husband's face she imagined when she dipped her finger into her folds. Today it was James Mortimer's dark eyes she pictured, his sensual mouth. The mouth that had lapped at her so scandalously. The right hand joined the left, her middle finger stroking, teasing, rubbing at the place at the apex of her thighs with growing urgency.

Heat bloomed in her chest, spreading to her toes and she kicked her blanket off in irritation, wishing she were naked after all, wishing she had another set of hands to tease at her nipples, wishing...

Wishing James was the one giving her pleasure.

She heard his voice, commanding her to let go.

The pulsing started deep within, in the place where her finger was buried, unfurling through her veins in glorious bursts of joy until it felt as if her whole body were spasming. It was magnificent, and went on and on, until finally it ebbed away like a sigh.

Out of breath, Carys stared at the ceiling without seeing anything. This, without a doubt, had been the best release she had ever brought on by herself. For a moment she toyed with the idea of resuming her caresses before realizing that she would be unable to. There wasn't an ounce of strength left in her body.

Exhausted, she let her arms flop onto the mattress—and fell asleep again.

∾

The first person Carys saw in the hall the following morning was Eirwen. As soon as she spotted her, her daughter came up to her, a frown on her face.

"Are you all right, Mam?"

"Yes, of course I am, lovely," Carys said, giving her cheek a stroke. "Why do you ask?"

"You look different."

Eirwen had always been very sensitive to other people's moods. It wasn't surprising therefore that she'd noticed something. But Carys could not discuss the reason for her unusual appearance with her daughter. She gave a little cough to hide her embarrassment.

"I slept so well I found it hard to wake up this morning. That may be why I look half asleep."

"You don't look half asleep, exactly."

No, she imagined she didn't. Flushed, rather. The pleasure she had not resisted in wringing from her grateful body before getting up would be responsible for it. Once again, imagining James' dark eyes and sinful mouth, she had brought herself to an explosive release. And apparently, it showed.

"Have you eaten yet?" she asked, reaching out to one of the bread loaves waiting on the table. Would the distraction work? It was worth a try.

"James Mortimer."

Carys' heart skipped a beat. She was used to her daughter's abrupt changes of topic during conversations but this time she couldn't help but feel Eirwen had guessed her mother's unusual attitude was linked to the handsome steward. Did Eirwen suspect what had come to pass between them? The fiery kiss, the scandalous encounter on the beach?

Lord, it did not bear thinking about.

"What about him?" she asked as calmly as she could.

"I like him. He's a good man. Yesterday, I stroked his dog. He smiled at me."

Smiled? Well. Carys' lips quivered. A rare favor, indeed.

Pensively, she chewed on her mouthful of bread. She already knew Branwen liked the man who had given Matthew the love he'd needed as a child. It pleased her to hear now that Eirwen liked James as well. It would make it easier when... Her brain ground to a halt. When what? He had made it quite clear he was not looking for anything. Or rather, that he was scared of being with someone because of his fears of fathering children, which was even worse.

It was not that he didn't want her, it was that he thought he couldn't be with anyone.

Before anything could happen, she had to put his mind at rest, tell him he had nothing to fear with her, because there was no chance she would ever fall with child, even if they slept together. She couldn't allow any misunderstanding to linger between them. Too much was at stake, they deserved to know where they stood before deciding anything. Say what he might, James wanted her. The way he had interrupted Richard the day before had to be a sign that he was not completely indifferent to her. Perhaps with the proper reassurance he might accept to give them a chance.

"Yes," she murmured to Eirwen, handing her a chunk of bread. "James Mortimer is a good man."

James could not believe what he was about to do.

He was about to tell Carys he wanted her to offer him a second chance if she'd have him. In other words, he was about to do what Richard had done the day before. Except, he would do it better. He would give her a kiss worthy of the name, leave her breathless, and make damn sure she did not refuse him.

But refuse him what, exactly? He did not feel ready to ask her for anything permanent, much less propose marriage. All he knew was that he sensed she had a role to play in his life, and he in hers. He felt in his bones he would regret it for the rest of his miserable life if he didn't at least try to behave as a normal man, a man who was not crippled by fear, would do.

He would not be a selfish coward anymore, could not afford to be, because the risk was too great. If he didn't find the strength to open up, he would lose her. And *that* was what frightened him most of all.

Axe in hand, he made his way back to the castle. Despite his intention to put his frustration to good use, he hadn't been able to prune a single tree. He felt as if he wouldn't be able to do anything, or think rationally, until he'd spoken to Carys and made sure she knew what was in his heart, doubts and all.

Once he'd replaced the tool back in the barbican, he headed toward the hall.

The door swung open before he could reach it and he found himself face to face with a woman—only, it was not the one he wanted to see.

Margaret?

His shock would not have been greater if he had seen the King of England standing in front of him. She was alone, and looking at him as if there was nothing more normal than for her to be at Sheridan Manor. Which was not his opinion at all.

"What are you doing here?"

"James, good morning to you, too," she said, making a point of remonstrating with him for his lack of manners.

"Good morning." Damn it all, he had no time for this! He needed to see Carys without delay. "What are you doing here? Did you travel on your own?" It would have been awfully risky for a woman to come from so far without a proper escort. What could have possessed her to even attempt it?

"No. I took the opportunity of following a family traveling north. They dropped me off in town earlier this morning." She shifted on her feet. "I'm here because there is a matter we need to discuss."

She looked so grave his heartbeat instantly picked up. "Is it Henry?" Had her only remaining son died in turn? Dear God, no. Was it a family curse? Was everyone he was related to, in some way or another, destined to die before their time? Margaret must have seen the panic flaring in his eyes because she instantly reassured him.

"No, Henry is well." She paused, and averted her eyes. "But what I have to say does concern a child of mine."

He arched a brow. As far as he knew, she only had one son left. That was the whole reason he had gone to her last summer, because she had lost almost everyone. So what the devil did she mean, another child of hers? He couldn't think. Unless... His eyes flicked to her stomach. Was she saying what he thought she was saying? Was she with child? Had she come to announce she had found herself another husband? Well, good luck to her, but he could not find it in himself to care one way or the other. He'd thought never to see her again, and it had suited him fine.

"Which child of yours?" he asked nonetheless.

There was another pause. Then she lifted her head and said the most shocking thing she could have said.

"Yours."

Chapter Eight

Fuck, fuck, *fuck!*

James rarely swore in his head, much less out loud, but if ever an occasion warranted it, this was it. He planted his axe in the birch in front of him, unleashing his fury on the hapless tree. Margaret was with child. *His* child.

A child who might die, like all the others.

Another swing of the axe separated a small branch from the tree trunk. As awful as it was, the fact that she was with child wasn't even the worst of it. He might have been able to push aside his fears long enough to calm down and remember that not all children died. But Margaret was carrying a child he didn't even remember conceiving. As far as he knew, the two of them had never slept together. So how was this possible? All day yesterday after leaving her in the bailey and all night he'd asked himself the same question, all morning he'd tried to find an answer as he hacked at the trees, without managing to come up with a single one.

Abandoning the axe, he slammed a fist into the oak to his left and howled when his skin split on the bark and pain reverberated all along his arm. Damn it all, he was too old to be so rash! Breaking his arm wouldn't help in any way.

"Fuck!" he exploded again, cradling his fist against his stomach. This was a disaster.

Because the biggest problem of all was not his fear of the baby dying, or the worrying memory lapse concerning its conception, it was the consequences Margaret's revelation would have on his life. If she was really carrying his child, then he would have to marry her. Which meant nothing could ever happen between him and Carys.

Fuck. This time the word didn't pass his lips. It only split his skull.

He couldn't be without her now, and he wasn't sure how he was going to survive this last, awful loss.

"Is there a problem?" a tentative voice, coming from behind him.

Yes. You could say that.

He turned to face Carys, who was looking at him with wide blue eyes. She had gone into the forest as she did most days, to forage for Avice. With her basket full of leaves and her green dress, she looked like a spring nymph, whereas with his dark clothes and bleeding hand he most likely resembled a demon from the underworld. In other words, they were two creatures that could never be reunited.

Damnation! Only the day before he had resolved to go to her and open up about his intentions regarding a possible future together. A moment later he had been told it would never happen, all because of a woman he did not want but might well have to marry and a babe he did not remember fathering, a child who had reawakened the fears he'd worked so hard to suppress.

Oh, the irony of it. Richard had once told him his story, how he'd been prevented from being with the woman he loved because he'd done his duty by the mother of his son instead, a woman he had bedded in a moment of boredom one summer, without really feeling anything for her.

Well, what was happening to him was even worse. He was not paying a hard price for having wanted to indulge his senses, and thought nothing of the consequences, he had done nothing he could claim to regret, because he did not even remember bedding Margaret.

The conception of this baby had to have happened when he was not aware of what he was doing, he had at least established that during his long, sleepless night. It was the only way to explain the fact that he didn't remember sleeping with his sister-in-law- and the only way to account for it. Had he been of sound mind, he would never have touched Joanne's younger sister. But if they had slept together while he was delirious with fever, he would have been unable to see the encounter for the mistake it was.

It was not difficult to imagine the scene. Margaret had come to tend to him during the night and he, startled by the appearance of a woman so near to him, fueled by a desire he'd suppressed for too long, unable to think with his head, had drawn her into his arms. Instead of trying to make him see reason, she had surrendered to his caresses, clumsy as they must have been. Hadn't he noticed that she seemed eager to woo him during his previous visit? She would have thought she'd won at last, maybe hoped he would agree to start a relationship with her.

It would have been a blow to realize in the morning that he had no recollection of what had happened, and no intention of staying with her. But it was hard to sympathize, for what else could she have expected? It would have been obvious he had no idea what he was doing while he bedded her.

No, she would have known deep down that it had meant nothing, save the slaking of an uncontrollable lust. Still, considering she'd been after his favors before their wild romp, he was surprised she had not tried to stop him when he'd left and only come back when she'd discovered she was with child.

Damn it all, to think he had stopped himself from taking Carys that day at the beach and every day since then because he was worried about losing control and getting her with child! And now, as a reward for his efforts, he was told he had fathered a child in a semi-conscious state, on a woman he didn't feel anything toward, and he had to live with the consequences, this on the day he'd decided to finally push his fears aside.

It was plain cruelty.

"Margaret, my sister-in-law is here," he said eventually, running his good hand through his hair.

"Yes. I heard she arrived yesterday." The look Carys threw him made it clear she was wondering why the news should send him into such a state.

"She is." Dear Lord, how was he to tell her the news? If, as he had cause to think, she had feelings for him and hopes for a future together, his declaration would be a blow. In the end he decided it was best to be blunt. She would be used to it by now. "She claims to be carrying my child."

Cary's face fell at the same time as his chest caved in. Having said the words out loud had made the situation he was facing all too real.

"I see." Her gaze flickered to his mangled hand. "And the prospect frightens you."

Frightened, horrified and angered him all at once. He didn't want to end his life as Margaret's husband. He didn't love her, or even feel any particular affection toward her. A few weeks ago he'd thought they would never set eyes on each other again and the prospect had suited him just fine. And more to the point, he'd had other plans, plans involving another woman.

A woman who looked as crestfallen as he felt. Fuck, he'd

been right, she *had* feelings and hopes, and she was struggling not express them, so as not to add to his burden.

Carys was struggling to absorb the news she'd just heard. James was going to be a father? She didn't know whether to be devastated on behalf of her poor heart, which had difficulty beating normally, or filled with pity for what he must be suffering right now. His bleeding hand and scowling face were enough to tell her he felt nothing like Matthew felt at the prospect of the imminent birth.

Then she stilled.

He'd said the woman "claimed" to be carrying his child. Which meant he had his doubts.

"You don't believe her claim?" She had to cling to the hope that this was a mistake that could be resolved somehow, because otherwise, it would be a disaster.

James hesitated, as if unsure whether to voice his concerns or not. In the end, to her relief, he seemed to conclude he could tell the truth because she wouldn't judge him.

"Honestly? I don't know what to think. She looks no different to her usual self, which doesn't help. It's only been four months since I left her cottage, of course, so it's possible she wouldn't be showing yet but..." Black eyes skewered her while he delivered the blow. "Here is what troubles me. I can't even remember bedding her. All I know is that whatever happened between us happened without my real consent and full knowledge. I was feverish for days on end while in her care and don't remember anything. I have no choice but to trust her word, and I'm not sure I want to, or can."

As declarations went, this one was rather shocking but Carys did her best not to react. James was having enough difficulty handling the news. He didn't need her to make him feel even worse.

He ran a hand through his hair again. There was stubble on

his jaw, betraying the fact he had not shaved that morning. Carys had rarely seen him so unkempt or agitated, would not even have believed he *could* get so agitated.

"Something feels odd. I know I would never have slept with her had I been in my right mind and find it hard to believe I would have wanted to, even when feverish... I've never felt any desire for her, or even really liked her, God forgive me. But considering the state I was in, there is no telling what I did. It's possible I did something so unlikely." He kicked the tree in front of him. "This is a nightmare, like being told you broke a bone slipping on a frozen lake when you can't recall having gone there in the first place and your arm is intact."

Yes. She could imagine it would be hard to accept. It was not an insignificant thing either. This lapse in judgment, if one could call it that, could have lifelong, potentially disastrous consequences. They had better make sure everything was as Margaret claimed. James was scared to death; she had to do what she could to help. She could not let him face this alone.

"Would you like me to go talk to her, see if I can find out a bit more?" she offered. "She doesn't know me, and has no idea that I know you. If I pretended I'm no one of importance and care not one way or another about what happens between you, she might allow me into her confidence."

James' eyes lit up for the first time since she had come to him that morning. The hope shining in them was enough to convince her she should speak to Margaret. If there was any way she could get him out of this nightmare, she had to try.

"You would do that?"

"Of course."

She would do so much more for him. As if he'd understood what she hadn't dared say, he took her hands in his and drew her close. "Thank you, Carys."

Oh, his name in his mouth! She willed her heartbeat down.

"Wait. It might not work, she might not be willing to confide in me," she cautioned, not wanting him to think his problem was solved. "Or I might find out that she is telling the truth."

That prospect was terrifying. Because then there would be no coming back. If the woman *was* indeed carrying his child, he would marry her, whatever his misgivings. A man of honor, he would not abandon her and the babe.

"No, I know. But it means a lot to me that you would even want to try to help." He leaned in toward her, all masculine intent. "You're the only one at Sheridan Manor I have told why Margaret is here. Matthew and Branwen have made her feel welcome, of course, but they do not know why she's here. They think she's only come for a visit. I didn't want to say anything until I was absolutely sure I knew where things stood."

It made sense. She nodded, overwhelmed by his proximity. "All right. Let me see what I can do."

The sooner they knew where they stood, the better.

"Carys, I—"

"No. Please." She stopped the declaration poised over James' lips and picked up the basket she had deposited at her feet, steeling her resolve. "We'll talk afterward."

If you're free to express your feelings then.

It didn't take Carys long to locate Margaret. Guessing the woman would be more at ease with the servants than with the lord and lady of the manor, she went straight to the kitchen and found her sitting by the fire, a cup in hand. She was laughing at John, the spit boy, who was doing his best to ignore her taunts.

James had described a small woman, with thin chestnut hair, a pointy face and a sallow complexion. He'd forgotten to mention however, that the result was somehow reminiscent of a mouse. The discovery only spurred Carys onward. A man like James Mortimer, who was a mighty eagle, if she'd ever seen one, could not end up married to a mouse.

As soon as she saw her enter, Avice took her to one side.

"Oh, my lady," she said, wringing her hands together. Carys let the undeserved greeting pass. No matter how many times she had told her friend she was not a lady, she was the master's wife's mother, and that was as good as anything for the cook. "Please help. I don't know what to do with the woman. She's getting herself in quite a state with the mead I foolishly offered her earlier. I dare not provoke Master James' anger by throwing his sister-in-law out of my kitchen, but really, she is disturbing everybody's work... Poor John is at his wits' end."

Carys allowed a grim smile to float on her lips. Margaret was in her cups? Even better, this could only serve her purpose. The woman might be more disposed to talk and not get suspicious so easily if she could not think straight. She did not let her conscience bother her. Every weapon at her disposal she would shamelessly use in her bid to establish the truth—and hopefully free James from a fate he dreaded.

"Leave it to me. I'll take her away from here."

"Would you?" Avice looked relieved. "Thank you, my lady."

"It's Carys to you," she reminded her, knowing it was in vain.

Then she turned to Margaret, who was reaching for the pitcher of mead, and plucked the cup from her hand before the woman could fill it up again.

"Come," she said firmly. "We'll leave these good people to work while we enjoy the sunshine outside. I was about to go for a stroll round the lists and I could do with some company. It's always good to meet new people, don't you think?"

To her relief, Margaret followed her without comment. She really was quite small, barely reaching to her chin, Carys observed, and rather scrawny. Next to James, who was at least a head taller than herself, she would look ridiculous. Not that it signified anything, of course, but still…

Wondering how best to broach the topic, Carys led her to the far end of the lists, toward the west tower. At first she commented on the various features of Sheridan Manor and the fine weather they'd been having of late. Then, once she was certain no one could hear them, she took a gamble.

"I understand you're James Mortimer's sister?"

Let's see how the woman would rectify the mistake. The wrong assumption might pique her ego and make her want to boast about her future with the castle steward. Margaret didn't disappoint. She giggled and took her arm as if they were the best of friends.

"You *are* mistaken, I'm afraid. I am his sister-in-law, and soon to be wife."

Well, that was clear enough. The woman did not doubt what would happen. But was she basing this on anything other than hope? That was the question.

"Congratulations." It was hard to infuse much warmth in the word when her mouth felt as if it had been filled with ash but Margaret didn't seem to notice anything. "Have you known each other long?"

Another giggle. Or rather another squeak. The woman really *was* just like a mouse. "I've known him for almost thirty years if you'll believe it. And I've been in love with him all this time. My sister met him thanks to me, and yet she was the one who got him in the end. How is that fair, you might ask? We looked very much alike, and our eyes were the exact same shade of blue. There was no reason for him to choose Joanne over me. If he wanted a blue-eyed wife, he could have had me."

What a stupid thing to say. As if the way one looked was all that mattered. What about the way one smiled, the way one talked? The warmth in their eyes, or lack thereof, when they looked at you, the sensuality in their gestures, the timbre of their voice? And that was even before you considered what was in their minds. Choosing a life partner was a decision based on much more important considerations than the color of their eyes. Margaret had to have drunk more mead than Carys had supposed if she could think things like that, much less utter them out loud.

Or perhaps she was just as unlikeable as James had hinted.

"I can understand why you might have fallen in love with him," was all she said.

This at least was no lie. Carys could well imagine falling for a man like James. Perhaps she had done more than imagine it. Perhaps she had already fallen for him. What else could explain her reaction when she'd been told she could never have him because he was going to marry another woman, a woman who was carrying his child?

Nothing.

Dear God, what a time to realize that you had fallen in love with someone, while she was talking to the woman who would be married to him before the week was out if she were indeed carrying his child.

"Do you know James then?" Margaret sounded delighted by the notion, as if this would only make her revelations more satisfying.

Know him... Carys bit her bottom lip. Yes, one could say that.

A memory of James ordering her to beg to be licked flashed through her mind. She ruthlessly forced it out.

"We have crossed paths on occasion."

Her whispered answer was brushed to the side as if unimportant. "He's everything a woman could wish for in a man, is he not? Tall, strong, with eyes that burn a path all the way from your breasts to your..." Instead of finishing the sentence, Margaret closed her eyes and gave a little moan. But Carys knew exactly where the heat of James' gaze could reach. The description was surprisingly accurate, even if she hated to admit it. "Dear, oh, dear. You don't meet men like him every day. The only way I could bear my husband's touch all these years was by imagining James' hands on me when he bedded me."

The conversation was making Carys increasingly uncomfortable but she pushed on. This was not about her, but about finding out what had happened while James had been ill and, the more she heard, the more suspicious she became. He was right. Something was odd.

Margaret leaned in to her, as if about to confide something. Carys forced herself not to recoil when the sickly smell of mead hit her nostrils. She couldn't betray her discomfort, not yet. "We slept together once more than twenty years ago, you know, the evening of my cousin's wedding. He thought I was Joanne and he fucked me so thoroughly I almost passed out with the pleasure of it."

Every single muscle in Carys' body seized up. The woman had tricked her sister's husband into sleeping with her? How? Did she even want to know? It could only be a sickening story, one that had nothing to do with what she was trying to find out, so she stayed silent. If she opened her mouth, her contempt would become too obvious to miss, even for a drunken woman, and Margaret would not utter another word.

How could she steer the conversation away from the woman's unsavory dealings and back to what had happened while James had been in her cottage? In the end, she didn't have to worry about it. Margaret was only too happy to gloat.

"I never forgot the pleasure he gave me that night so when he came to see me back in the summer, I thought I would die with happiness." She sighed. "But he didn't seem interested in what I had to offer. Fortunately, he fell ill before he could leave for good. I could not believe my luck. Having him naked and all to myself in a bed night and day was the best thing that could have happened to me."

The best thing? James had gone to her because two of her children had died in tragic circumstances. Then he had been so ill he'd fought for his life. And all Margaret could think was that she'd had him all to herself in bed. Carys thought she might be sick. What had the woman done while he lay at her mercy? It was little wonder James didn't remember sleeping with his sister-in-law if Margaret had stroked him while he was unconscious and taken her pleasure without his knowledge or consent.

Was it even possible to make love to a man in such a state? To get him aroused physically while his mind could not fight the physical sensations, enough to allow intercourse to happen? She had no idea and, in truth, the less she thought about it, the better.

Bile in her throat, she waited for the rest of the distasteful story.

"I hoped when Joanne died that he might find comfort in my arms. I was freshly widowed myself then, and all available. But he never even came to see me. I suppose he took advantage of his new freedom to sleep with all the women in the county."

Carys knew he had done no such thing. He would have been grieving a wife he had loved deeply and too scared of fathering children to even think of going to a woman but she kept her comments to herself. She was finally getting to the heart of the matter, now was not the time to scare Margaret away.

"So I could not believe my luck when he actually visited me after being told about my children's death. I had feared never to see him again. I tried to entice him into staying for good while he helped my son Henry build the barn, but he didn't seem to notice my interest, or if he did, he pretended he did not." A snort, betraying her displeasure. "Then finally, fate decided I deserved more than being ignored and made sure I got the opportunity to spend more time with him."

"You mean, by striking him down with a fever that nearly killed him?"

The sarcasm was utterly lost on Margaret, who smiled a beatific smile. "Yes. It was the perfect opportunity to ensure I had unlimited access to his body." Her eyes became dreamy and Carys could not repress a shudder. What had the depraved woman done? She disentangled her arm from Margaret's, finding it unbearable to touch someone who thought nothing of preying on vulnerable men. "After I nursed him back to health, I thought he would see that I could make him happy but he left as soon as he was able to, with barely a thank you. So, in the end, I had no choice but to come up with a plan. I refuse to wait another thirty years for him, do you hear? I don't see why I should have to."

Carys wanted to flee before she heard sordid details that might push her over the edge but she could not give up now, not when she was too close to finding out the truth.

"What plan did you come up with?" she forced herself to ask. "It must have been a clever one."

The flattery worked. Margaret simpered and took her arm again. "It was. James will marry me if he thinks I am carrying his child. He's too honorable to refuse me and the babe his protection. He's not to know he was unable to actually reach his release while ill with the fever, only hard enough to allow me to reach mine."

Carys' heart skipped a beat when hope surged through her. Had she heard right? Pushing the image of a naked Margaret riding an unsuspecting James to the back of her mind, she asked, desperate to make sure she had not misunderstood. "You mean you're not really with child?"

There was another of Margaret's awful squeaky giggles. Why the woman thought the situation was funny in any way was beyond her.

"Not at the moment, no. But once we are married, I suspect it won't be long before I give him a son. I'm still young enough and I will make sure he fills me up with his seed time and time again. With a man so virile in my bed, it shouldn't take long for my womb to quicken."

"No, it should not." Carys had no idea how she had not retched yet. "But how are you going to explain to him that your body is not changing in the next few weeks? Won't he get suspicious?"

It had already been more than four months since James had left her house. Next month she would be halfway through her supposed pregnancy. It would not be long before he started asking questions. As he already had doubts, he might decide to wait until he could see with his own eyes he was going to be a father.

Margaret shrugged, as if that were of no importance whatsoever rather than the crux of the matter. "I will just tell him once we are married that I lost the babe. It happens. It won't matter anyway, as by then I will be his wife. It will be too late for him to change his mind."

Carys was now not simply disgusted, she was horrified. The deception was awful to play on any man. On James, who was mortally afraid of losing another child, it was just plain cruel. Forget the lies, the trick played on him and Joanne that night all those years ago, the taking advantage of him in a vulnerable state, the anguish she had cost him with her lie.

This was what he would never forgive Margaret. With reason.

Having heard all she wanted to hear, Carys led Margaret to a bench and forced her to sit down before she hurried back toward the gate. She had to see James now, and put an end to his agony, tell him that he didn't have anything to fear. He was not going to be a father.

And he would never have to marry Margaret.

Chapter Nine

"You were right. She's not with child."

James was in the weapon room by the barbican, sharpening an axe when Carys finally located him. He dropped everything when she said the words he would have been hoping to hear and turned to face her. His eyes were two glittering gems, and the heat burning in them reached, just like that wretched Margaret had said earlier, all the way to her core. For a moment she wondered if, in his relief, he would kiss her. He did not, instead taking her by the arm.

"Come."

He led her to a small room at the back of the stables. His personal room, she realized when she saw the three black tunics that had been placed to dry on the chest in the corner and the blanket they had used that day on the beach.

At any other time she might have found herself both unnerved and aroused by the memory—and the proximity of his bed. But right now she just wanted to share what she had learned during her conversation with his conniving sister-in-law.

He closed the door behind them and lifted his chin. "Tell me all."

Carys bit her lip. No, not all. She would not reveal the full extent of the woman's treachery, as it would cause him unnecessary pain and humiliation. He would not be told that Margaret had tricked him into sleeping with her all those years ago. He only needed to know that he didn't have to marry a woman he didn't want because she was not with child. Would she be strong enough to hide anything from him? She wasn't sure, as she had never been able to dissemble, and a man like him would be able to wiggle information out of anyone, but she had to try.

His attitude did not help her hold on to her composure. He had never looked more forbidding. With his back ramrod straight, his nostrils flaring, his eyes flashing in anger, he was truly formidable.

"Luck was with me," she started without further ado. The important thing was to put an end to his agony. "She was full of mead when I found her and all too ready to talk to a stranger. I think she relished the chance to expose what she saw as a clever plan and quickly confirmed what you suspected. She is not with child."

The spark of ire in James' eyes was instantly doused. His whole body finally relaxed, as if he'd not dared to hope until he'd heard her repeat the words.

"So she lied about us sharing a bed? About us..." He stopped and made what would have been a grimace in another man.

"N-not exactly," Carys murmured. Oh, this was excruciating. Why did she have to be the one announcing such news to him? "I'm afraid she did share your bed, in more ways than one. Don't you have any memories of her coming to lie next to you, of touching you?"

How many times had the woman used him for her pleasure? Probably more than once.

James frowned. "She was constantly by my side, that much I remember, feeding me, wiping my brow, my chest, to bring the temperature down..."

His voice trailed. It was clear he was remembering Margaret lingering over the gesture, and maybe more. Carys' stomach roiled. James' sister-in-law might not have gotten with child from the abuse she'd visited on him, but she had most definitely done all that was needed to have him while he lay at her mercy. There was no prize for guessing how she would have roused his body so that she could take her pleasure with him.

"I'm sorry. It's not what anyone would want to hear."

As she apologized, a thought struck her. James had said his illness had been severe and he'd found it unusually hard to shake off the fever. What if there had been more to it than a simple seasonal chill? What if Margaret had prolonged his weakness with herbs and potions so that she could enjoy his body for longer? After what Carys had heard, she wouldn't put anything past the woman.

She kept her doubts to herself, however, and hoped James had not started wondering the same thing. He would feel soiled enough already, what good would it do to be told he might have been kept at the woman's mercy for longer than necessary?

"She said she'd always been in love with you, even before your wedding to Joanne, and had hoped you would marry her instead of her sister. That is why she concocted this mad plan."

What was she doing? Why had she felt the need to add this? As if anything could justify the woman's actions!

James stared ahead of him, stunned by all he'd just heard.

Margaret was in love with him. She'd taken advantage of his weakened state to have her way with him. She'd lied about carrying his child when she knew he was mortally afraid of losing another babe. She had tried to force him into a union he didn't desire and ruin the rest of his life.

Though it was a lot to take in, he did not for a moment think to doubt Carys was telling the truth. He'd thought from the start that there was something wrong with this story, and worse, he'd started to have disturbing memories in the last few weeks, memories he'd done his best to push to the back of his mind.

Heat pooling in his groin, hair brushing against his stomach, hands roaming all over his body. A woman moaning above him.

"Dear God," he whispered, feeling all the blood drain from his veins.

It had not been just a nightmare, or visions brought on by fever. It had been real.

He'd started to wonder if there wasn't a problem with Margaret while he'd stayed in her cottage. There had been an odd gleam in her eyes every time she'd addressed him. It had made him uncomfortable and he'd done his best to convince himself that he was imagining things, going as far as thinking himself perverted for attributing such thoughts to his sister-in-law. Her change of attitude could have all too easily be attributed to grief, which, he knew, could cause a person to act oddly.

But now he was told she'd been in love with him all along and he had not imagined the lewd scenes happening under the cover of darkness.

How could she have taken advantage of him thus? What was he to think? Had the loss of her children unhinged her mind? It would explain why she had done such an outrageous thing as to violate his body while he was unable to stop her or even understand what was happening.

"I think you should beware. I'm sorry to say she is prepared to go quite far in her bid to have you."

Carys' words brought him back to the present.

"Yes. So I see." If she had been prepared to rape him and then lie about being with child to force him into marriage, everything was possible. "But did she really think I would not notice her body was not changing?"

A pause. "I think she didn't think that far ahead. She only wanted to secure your hand. The rest did not matter."

He understood from the way Carys averted her eyes that she was keeping something from him. It came to him in a flash of understanding. Once her position was secure, Margaret would have pretended to lose the child, thereby destroying what little sanity he had left. He swallowed, loving Carys for trying to spare him the full horror of his sister-in-law's scheme. As a thank you for her efforts, he pretended he had not guessed it anyway.

"I'm sorry. It cannot have been easy for you to hear the depth of her depravity."

It would have been horrifying. The only consolation was that it had been this way around. He would surely have gone mad if *he'd* had to hear about someone raping Carys while she was unconscious.

She gave him a taut smile that told him all he needed to know about what she had thought of Margaret's confession. "Don't worry about me."

But he did worry. No one should have to hear such sordid tales about people they cared about. Because in this moment, he felt sure she cared about him as much as he cared about her. And thanks to her, he was once again free to speak about his feelings and intentions for the future. Could he do it now?

No. He had to do things in order.

James closed the gap between them and placed a hand over her cheek, forcing himself to stay still when he wanted to draw her into a kiss. "Will you be all right here, waiting for me a moment?"

"Yes."

Before he could do anything, he was going to have a discussion with Margaret.

~

"You whore!"

James froze when Margaret's insult scalded his ears. Not her! And especially not now, when he was about to kiss Carys. His fingers tightened into her soft hair, frustration radiating through his every bone. His lips were an inch away from her mouth, his heart was thumping hard in his chest, and he had to stop and see to a woman he wished never to see again.

Would there be no end to the trouble Margaret caused him?

As soon as he had finished talking to her, he had run back to Carys, to tell her that it was all over. Thanks to her, he wouldn't have to marry a woman he didn't want. The relief had been so overwhelming he had drawn her into his arms to do what he had been prevented from doing the day before. She had not pulled away, rather looked at him with eyes aglow with hope and desire. The temptation had been impossible to resist. They were alone in his room, and there was a bed behind them.

He would kiss her, then he would take her to bed.

For once, he didn't want to think, to fear, or worry about the consequences. Carys knew what he feared so he trusted she would help him stay in control when the moment came. In any case, it was either risk it or go mad with frustration. Having escaped Margaret's clutches, he felt reborn. Having been told what she had done, he felt the need to cleanse himself.

Carys would be the one to do that for him.

They had been about to kiss when the door to his bedchamber had burst open, allowing an irate Margaret into the room. Damnation! How had she known where to find them? Had she followed him after their discussion, then waited, listening at the door? If she had, she would have heard everything, and understood what he and Carys were about to do.

When he turned to face her, Margaret didn't spare him a glance. She was glaring at Carys as you would to an enemy, her eyes burning with an unholy fire. "You whore! You told him what I did, didn't you, you turned him against—"

"There is only one whore in this room," James cut in, his voice like ice. "And it is not Carys. You had better remember it before I gag you."

"This is all her fault. You were going to marry me and now—"

"I would never have married you." Was she really so deluded? "I sensed there was something not right with your story. I would have waited for your belly to swell to decide anything and it wouldn't have taken me long to see that there was no child, and therefore no reason for us to marry."

She completely ignored him and turned her attention back to Carys, who had taken a few steps back. "You wanted him for yourself, you bitch! You were jealous I was going to get him. Well, if I can't have him, then, neither can you."

With those words, Margaret drew a knife out of her sleeve and launched herself at Carys. There was no time to think. James threw himself between the two women, desperate to stop the murder of an innocent. Seeing she was going to be stopped, Margaret changed tack and swung her arm in a wide arc. There was no avoiding the cut. The knife caught him on the cheek, slicing at his flesh, but he barely registered the pain, too intent on neutralizing her without breaking her arm. Fury was lending Margaret more strength than he would have thought possible. Still, she was too small, and ultimately no match for him. If she was determined to kill, he was twice as determined to survive.

The knife fell to the floor with a *clang*. He kicked it to the other end of the room, where she wouldn't be able to retrieve it.

Margaret did not stop struggling, however. Taking advantage of James' resolve not to hurt her, she wiggled like a worm, making it impossible for him to hold her in place. She roared, clawed at his face, did her best to bite whatever part of him she could reach. There was no other choice but to stun her. He could not risk having her launch herself at someone else when she left the room a defeated woman only to hurt another innocent. In the state she was in, she might even cause herself harm. His blow caught her just under the chin.

She dropped like a stone, the silence in the room deafening after the mad struggle.

James let out a sigh of relief.

"Go get help," he instructed Carys, kneeling by the unconscious woman. He could not go himself, in case Margaret came to while he was gone. He needed to be the one to face her if she started to lash out again.

Carys nodded and ran to the barbican, not thinking for a moment to argue. The scene she had just witnessed had been terrifying. Who would have thought a woman as small in stature as Margaret would struggle so fiercely? It had been obvious James had done his best to control her without inflicting any pain. Considering what the woman had done to him, she thought his restraint commendable. In the end, though, he'd had no choice but to stun her.

It had been the quickest, safest solution.

When she came back a moment later accompanied by three of the guards, she found James standing by the window, looking as calm as if nothing of importance had happened. His profile, carved against the whitewashed walls, was heartbreakingly beautiful, his dark skin offering a striking contrast to the paleness of the background.

His orders were delivered to the men in his flat, matter-of-fact voice.

"Please take my sister-in-law away. I'm sorry to say that she attacked her ladyship's mother for no reason that we can discern." He sighed, as if pained by this development. Carys of course knew better. "I had no other choice but to stun her to stop her from injuring herself. She will need to be put under lock and key, for fear she tries to hurt someone else. Do not let her sway you with her bile when she wakes up. Ignore what she says. She lost her children recently and I think she is not in her right mind, as can be evidenced for this unwarranted attack."

The tallest of the men gestured to the other two that they should carry her between them. "Of course. You can be sure she won't escape until you have decided what to do with her."

"Thank you." James carried on staring straight ahead, not sparing them or his sister-in-law a glance.

The three men left, a limp Margaret with them. Carys could not find it in herself to pity the woman. After all she had done, she deserved nothing less than to be locked in a room to reflect on her perfidy. Once they were alone, James left his place by the window to come stand in the middle of the room. All the air left her lungs.

"Dear God, but you're bleeding!" she cried out, running to him.

There was a cut on his cheek, just below the eye. How had she not seen it before? The whole left side of his face was covered in blood. It was a horrific sight but James placed a finger on his cheek and shrugged.

"'Tis nothing."

No, perhaps not compared to what it could have been, but it was still bad enough. It wasn't very deep but it was as long as her index finger. "It's going to require stitches," she said, feeling close to swooning, a most unusual reaction for her. She was not one to faint at the sight of blood. So why was she so unsettled?

"Sit down," James ordered when she wavered.

As her legs were about to give way from under her, she was only too glad to comply. A stool was conveniently placed behind her and she fell rather than she sat on it. In a dazed state, Carys watched as James went to find a needle, some thread, a square piece of linen and a pitcher of water. His gestures slow and measured, he placed everything on the table next to where she was. Then he squatted in front of her, his hands on her knees.

"I've seen your embroidery. It's exceptionally good."

"I-is it?" she stammered. Why on earth was he talking about this now? Embroidery? What did it have to do with any of this?

"It is. And so I would like you to stitch me up. Old Agnes' sight is going and I fear she will only butcher me. Much better to have someone skilled with a needle to see to my wound, don't you think?"

Her heart skipped a beat at the idea of stitching him. Say what he might, this was nothing like embroidery, and she was already feeling lightheaded. Could she do what he was asking in such conditions?

"Mistress Ivy in the village is also a skilled healer and her sight is fine," she croaked. "We could send someone to her and—"

The hands at her knees slid higher, silencing her. She could feel the heat of his palms through the material of her dress. "Please, Carys. No old Agnes, no Mistress Ivy. No other healer I don't know. I want you."

Though she knew what he'd meant to say, the words sounded like a declaration. He wanted her, in more ways than one. Her heart started to beat a fierce rhythm, because she wanted him too, in more ways than one.

"If you're sure." The words had difficulty passing her mouth.

"I'm sure."

"Then it's your turn to sit down."

With a smile, he straightened back up and helped her to her feet. Fingers entwined, they stared at each other a long moment. Was he about to kiss her? Her heart started to beat wildly in anticipation, but he shook his head slightly, as if to say he would not touch her, not while his face was covered in blood.

Forcing herself to be grateful for this mark of consideration rather than dwell on her disappointment, Carys walked over to the table where everything was waiting for her. When she turned around, James took his position on the stool, then lifted his head up in readiness.

She approached on legs that felt barely able to support her. His eyes were burning with feverish intent and appeared darker than ever. Dear, oh dear. It seemed every time she thought she'd seen him at his most forbidding, something happened to make her see how wrong she'd been. Was there no end to the depth of his intensity? Thank the Lord he was only half Egyptian. More masculine power might well have paralyzed her.

"Do your worst. Only, don't get carried away and transform the scar into a flower, or heaven forbid, a robin. It wouldn't be very manly."

His words teased a smile out of her. How could he jest at a time like this? But she was grateful for it, as it helped ease the tension in her body. She needed to be relaxed to do this. "No robin, I promise. But before I do anything, I'm going to clean the wound."

"Of course. What was I thinking? The easy part first."

Carys nodded. He was right. The cleaning would be easy, and even pleasurable. For both of them. They had better enjoy it because then the torture would begin. For both of them. With tender gestures, she wiped his cheek, jaw, and neck. As she'd already noticed this morning, he hadn't shaved. White specks peppered the otherwise black stubble, especially on the chin and around the mouth. It was fascinating, and by the time she had finished, she was certain she had not cleaned anyone so thoroughly.

Eventually, she could not stall any longer. The bloodied cloth was discarded and she applied herself to the task of fitting the thread through the eye needle, a task made harder than it should have been by her trembling hands. Holding the needle at the ready she turned to him.

"Ready?"

"I think I'm readier than you are." He eyed her hand with an arched brow.

"Possibly. This is nothing like embroidery. I have not sewn up many wounds in my time, and every time was worse than the previous one."

"Let us hope that it is the last time you have to do it, then."

"Indeed," Carys replied fervently.

The first stitch caused her breath to hitch in her throat. The second made her stomach roil. The last one cost her every ounce of determination she had left. By the time she cut the thread, she was barely able to stand. Ever mindful of her well-being, James drew her to him, keeping her upright with an arm around the waist.

"Don't go falling now," he chided, his voice gentle. "If you cracked your skull, I wouldn't know what to do."

"If I cracked my skull, I'm not sure there would be anything *to* do."

Carys gave a shaky laugh, relieved it was all over. Why had she been so affected by a measly three stitches? She had once stitched a cut on her own knee without flinching, despite the pain. So why did she feel on the verge of a swoon for piercing someone else's skin? She hadn't been the one suffering.

Because the skin you've pierced was James' her mind screamed at her, *and you feel more for him than you have felt for anyone since Dewi.*

"Thank you, Carys," James said with his mouth against her arm. She suspected he was fighting the urge to place his lips on her breast, which was exactly at the right height to allow him to do that, and she closed her eyes. How she longed to feel his mouth on this part of her! Giving herself pleasure was one thing, and she could stroke the little sensitive bud hidden in her folds as efficiently as anyone. But nothing she could do replaced the feel of a man suckling at her, of his tongue lapping at her nipple, drawing it deep into his hot mouth, making it hard and then soothing the burn with long, delicious pulls.

Go drapia, this had to stop! Oh well, at least she hadn't spoken out loud this time. She hoped.

Shaking, she took a step back and almost tripped on the hem of her skirt.

"Don't thank me. Just make sure it doesn't happen again."

It was a ridiculous thing to say. No one could guarantee they would never be hurt, and he had not asked to be attacked. Nevertheless, James didn't point it out. Instead he said, "I can at least promise I will not let Margaret hurt you ever again."

Never had he sounded more determined. And this determination was on her behalf. Carys swallowed back a sob.

"It is my turn to thank you. That strike was intended for m-me," she stammered, as the truth slammed in. Had he not stepped in front of her so decisively, the knife would have cut *her*, perhaps on the side of the neck, perhaps in the eye. She might not have survived the attack.

"Yes, that strike was meant for you, and it was supposed to do much more than slash your cheek," James snapped, shooting back to his feet. "How can you even suppose I could have let such a thing happen? Margaret only wanted to punish you for helping me but you did nothing wrong and shouldn't have to pay for giving me my life back. How could I have lived with myself if anything had happened to you?"

"Nothing happened," she replied, taken aback by his vehemence. "It's all right."

And then it hit her. If *she* could have been killed, then so could he. This could have been much worse than a cut to the cheek. This time she did stumble.

James let out a muffled curse. Thank God it was all over. Even with Carys' soft touch, the stitching of his wound had been excruciating. He should make Margaret pay not for the pain she had inflicted on him, but for the ordeal it had been for Carys to see to the cut. Even now, though it was over, her hands were shaking so much she almost dropped the cup of ale he had poured her.

"You could have died," he heard her say to herself. Thank God for her habit of talking to herself. He'd thought she was still recovering from having had to stitch him up, when in fact she was fretting over what could have happened to him. He hated it, hated the idea of her being unsettled in any way, especially through his fault.

"Nonsense," he said roundly. "Get that silly idea out of your head." The bluntness seemed to have the desired effect. Thank God she was no impressionable little miss but a woman of sense. Instead of wasting time being offended she nodded, as if his words had restored her to her senses.

"No, you're right. You didn't die. I should stop being so silly," she muttered, before applying herself to the task of emptying the cup he'd given her. He took a long sip from his own drink while he waited for her to resume the conversation. It wasn't long before she did. "So, what will happen to Margaret now? Will you tell Matthew and Branwen what she did? And why she came?"

"No." It wouldn't serve any purpose. The fewer people knew about what had happened in that cottage, the better. "I will take her back to her son Henry and wash my hands of her.

He is the only family she has left. He will have to take care of her. I will not lift a finger to help her."

"No. No one can expect it of you after what she did."

She meant what she had done to *him*, raping him then forcing him to face his worst nightmare. But, as bad as that was, he resented Margaret more for having wanted to kill Carys than for playing the awful deception on him.

The rest of his drink was emptied in one gulp and he walked over to the window when the truth hit him. She could have died today. Dear God, forget him, *she* could have died. How would he have survived it?

"Get that silly nonsense out of your head." Carys' voice, unusually stern, came from behind him. Was she trying to imitate his earlier tone? It sounded like it. "I didn't die."

No, she had not, thank heaven.

He turned to face her, panic receding. It was over, and fretting about what might have happened would accomplish nothing.

Carys smiled and brushed a light hand along his wound.

"Dewi had a scar in the exact same place, you know." For a moment she appeared lost in remembrance and there was a glazed look in her eyes he had never seen before. She always was so focused on what she was doing, so busy enjoying herself to the full that it disconcerted him.

"And here I was, thinking I was the only man ever to come to your aid," James said, hoping to distract her from thoughts of her late husband. Not that he was jealous, exactly, but he would rather have her thinking of him while she was touching him, a normal reaction, he was sure everyone would agree.

"You are the only man to have ever stepped between me and an attacker," she assured him with a smile. "Dewi got his scar cantering through the forest. Too busy worrying about how I was coping with the speed, he didn't pay attention to where he was going and a branch hit him. Much less chivalrous than stopping someone from stabbing me, admittedly. But I kept telling him it gave him a dangerous air."

There was such tenderness in her eyes that his throat constricted. How good it was to be loved thus, to have someone to make you feel special every day. He missed it almost as much as he missed Joanne herself. It was the best feeling in the world.

"I'm sure he would have defended you as I did, given the opportunity." Suddenly he wasn't jealous, he just wanted Carys to remember how cherished being married to Dewi had made her feel. And the man sounded like a good man, worried more about how his wife was faring than his own safety. He would have known she was a nervous rider and thought to look after her. "Unfortunately for him, Wales seems to lack deranged women ready to stab people who have done nothing to deserve it."

"Yes. I'm sure he would have defended me." She gave him a grateful smile for saying so. "And we could certainly find such women in Wales. Our two countries are not so different, you know."

"No, I already suspected as much."

But even if it had been different, how could he blame anyone for their origins when he had suffered from prejudice himself?

"I need to wipe your cheek, the stitching made you bleed again," Carys said softly.

Without waiting for his agreement, she went to retrieve the piece of cloth from the table. At her nod, he sat back down on the stool. It amused him to think he was too tall for her to be able to tend to his cheek comfortably if he remained standing.

"Don't move."

Oh, he had no intention of going anywhere. The cold cloth against his skin was soothing and Carys' proximity did wonderful things to his insides. Now that the ordeal was over, James found himself wondering why he had he not thought of injuring himself before. Nothing too drastic, of course, a small cut to the chin, or a slash on the wrist. Because having her look after him was a pleasure like no other.

Then he remembered that he had only been cut because he'd taken a blow destined to kill Carys, and his mood darkened again. What on earth had possessed Margaret to do such a thing as murder another woman? Was her supposed love for him enough to justify the desperate act? Of course not. Was she truly deranged then, as he'd started to suspect? Perhaps. But for all the lies and deception, he could not ignore that she had seemed to know what she was talking about where he was concerned.

"There is something I don't understand," he said while Carys dipped the bloodied cloth in the bowl of water to rinse it.

During their conversation, in her bid to convince him of her sincerity, Margaret had revealed details about his anatomy, details only someone who had been intimate with him could know. She had looked after him for days, had had plenty of opportunity to see him naked and had even, to his everlasting horror, taken possession of his body, so perhaps he shouldn't be surprised she knew what he looked like without clothes on. But she had also known how he behaved when he had a woman in his arms, the sounds he made, the kind of encouragements he gave. How could she know that if she'd only taken advantage of his unconscious state? Was he missing something? Had he made love to her willingly before falling ill, only to have the memory of it wiped out by the fever?

It had to be the case because what she had described could only have happened if he was fully conscious—and eager.

"I know I said I did not make love to her willingly while I

was racked with fever, and I stand by it, but there were things Margaret couldn't have known unless we had actually..."

The words trailed off when Carys stilled and averted her gaze. His insides went liquid. She knew something.

Something he would hate to hear.

"Carys?" He had to know, whatever it was.

"Forgive me, I wasn't going to tell you."

"No. But now you are," he said, taking hold of her wrist and forcing her to look at him. The cleaning of his wound could wait. This could not. He needed to know what had happened between him and his sister-in-law or he would drive himself mad trying to remember. "Tell me now. Please."

Carys must have seen the desperation in his eyes because she nodded slowly.

"During our conversation she confirmed that she was not with child, but she also revealed very disturbing details about your past life."

Past life? He frowned.

"You mean she didn't take advantage of my illness?" Had he got it wrong?

"No, I'm sorry, she made it quite clear she did. You did not want her in your arms, or even know what was happening, she admitted as much. Then she bemoaned the fact that she could not bring you to... well, you know..."

He cut her fumbled explanation short. "I see. She got my body aroused, enough to use it for her pleasure, but she could not get me to release my seed and make her with child," he clarified in his usual, blunt manner. He had *not* imagined the heat of her mouth around him, then. Jesus.

"Yes." Another pause. His whole body tensed. What Carys was about to reveal would be bad, he could feel it. "She also told me you had slept together once before, years ago, without your knowledge."

Without his knowledge? He had never suffered from a fever such as the one that had floored him in the winter, and he never drank to excess. How on earth could he have made love to his sister-in-law and not known it? "I... Are you certain?"

Had she misunderstood? How could two conscious people sleep together without both of them knowing what was happening?

Carys bit her bottom lip. "Yes. I'm sorry, this is difficult for me."

It would be, but he had to know and she was the only one who could help. There was no way he could ask Margaret. "I understand. But please tell me. All of it. Don't try to spare me. I need to know."

A nod. "She and Joanne looked quite similar from what I understand."

Well, yes, broadly speaking, they had. Many people had commented on the resemblance over the years but to him, there had always been a crucial difference between the two sisters, one that made it impossible for him to see them in the same light. Joanne's petite features had added to her charm, whereas Margaret's bitterness had made her already small face appear pinched. Though the two animals could have been described in a very similar manner, no one would ever think of comparing a squirrel to a rat, would they? In his mind, the two women had been as different as night from day.

Now was not the time to point it out, however. They were discussing what Margaret had done.

"Yes, they did," he said.

When he lifted his chin, Carys carried on. "She confided she had tricked you into sleeping with her, or rather that she had not rectified your mistake when you mistook her for Joanne one night."

"Mistake her?" How in the name of all that was holy would

he mistake his beloved wife for another woman and not know the difference? He waited while Carys gathered the courage to speak because he could not think of a single explanation.

"She said something about her cousin's wedding."

His insides, which had somehow recovered from realizing Carys had revelations to make, dissolved again, this time completely.

Oh, God.

The wedding. The tryst by the pond later in the evening... That had been Margaret?

He remembered the encounter well enough, even if he'd drunk more than usual. After a whole day of revelry he had gone to relieve himself behind a hedge by the village pond and ended up making love to Joanne on the mossy ground.

Except... except now he was told it had not been her at all.

Feeling unsettled by the whole episode, he had never dared mention it to Joanne afterward and she had never alluded to it either. Now he understood why. Because she had not been the woman kneeling at his feet in the darkness and begging to be taken there and then. That bold behavior had been out of character for his wife, there was no denying it. He'd put it all down to the heat of the moment, and the quantity of mead she had consumed, but it had not stopped him from feeling guilty. That night he had been unusually vigorous. And the woman on all fours in front of him unusually wild.

Now he knew why.

How had he not suspected something was not right? He should have guessed... But how could he have imagined anyone other than his wife would have come to him, demanding to be taken? It had been a moonless night and, in the darkness, nothing he'd seen had been enough to raise his suspicion. The hair he'd fisted while she'd pleasured him had been the exact same shade of brown he expected it to be, the hips he had grabbed as he'd pumped into her had been just as slender as the ones he was used to.

Fury, shame, disgust, slammed into him. What had Margaret done? What had she made him do that night? Thank God he had not said anything about the encounter to Joanne because questions would have been raised. It would not have taken them long to find out what had really happened but it was better his wife had gone to her grave never knowing her sister had betrayed her so.

"I'm sorry, I can't tell you much more, as I didn't ask for any details," Carys said, mistaking his reaction for confusion. She thought he had no idea what night Margaret was talking about. He didn't tell her that, unfortunately, he knew all too well. It was humiliating enough as it was. "As soon as I'd heard what I needed to reassure you, I left. I found the whole conversation distasteful in the extreme."

Yes. As anyone would. Would there be no end to his sister-in-law's depravity? He'd thought her mind had been addled by the shock of her children's death but if she had already done such an outrageous thing as to let him take her when he was convinced he was making love to his wife, then he could seriously doubt her sanity. That encounter had taken place more than twenty years ago. Had she been mad all this time?

Dear God. He hated her for making him feel he had betrayed Joanne.

"Let me finish cleaning the blood now," Carys said gently.

Yes. If only she could also clean the guilt and shame away.

Chapter Ten

"Are you leaving already?"

Carys understood she had spoken out loud again when James gave a side smile. He was carrying a blanket and what looked like provisions for the road. Had he come to say goodbye before taking Margaret home? Was that what it was?

Her stupid heart skipped a beat at the idea of watching him ride away. Foolishly, she had hoped he would come to his senses and ask someone else to take his sister-in-law home. Of course, he would do no such thing. He would consider it his duty to see her safe. Regardless of what she had done, she was Joanne's sister. That was enough to ensure his protection. After what had happened, there was no chance he would stay in her village, much less in her cottage, but still the idea of him going away disturbed Carys. What if he fell ill again and never recovered? What if he met someone while he was away? What if he—

"No, I'm not leaving today. Margaret will have to spend another day as her prisoner in her room because before I go, there is something I need to do. It's most important."

"Oh?"

Carys berated herself for the most uninspired answer in the world but she did not seem to have the presence of mind to say anything else. Fortunately, James didn't seem to mind her lack of originality, or even notice it.

"Yes." He gestured to the items in his hands. "I'm taking you to the beach."

It was not a question, but a statement. And there was only one thing she could answer.

"Yes. Please."

A moment later, they were gone.

Without even discussing the possible options, they took the same horses they had taken the other day, and went to the same spot in the bay. It was a glorious day. The sky stretched above them, as blue as she imagined Heaven might be, and the water appeared to have been strewn with a myriad of sparkling diamonds. The beauty of the scene made Carys' heart sing. Why had she waited so long to discover the sea? She already knew it would be a long-lasting passion of hers and she would be back as often as she could.

Disbelief made her shake her head. Was she really falling for something new so late in life? It would appear so.

The thought, inevitably, made her look at James, who was tying the horses to the same cluster of trees they had used the first time they had come and everything within her bloomed.

Yes, perhaps she *was* falling in love.

It was different from what had happened with Dewi. With her husband, she had known from the start they were made for each other. She had not asked herself any questions, not wondered if being with him was a good idea or if he shared her feelings. There had been no hesitation about what the future might bring for them, no self-doubting. For someone who had been a somewhat shy child, it had been a liberation to be certain of something for once, and simply act on it. Rushing headlong into the relationship with the impetuosity of youth had been the obvious thing to do. And during their marriage, Dewi had allowed her to blossom into the confident, mature woman she was now.

Being with a man who loved her no matter what she did or said had freed her in more ways than one and, decades later, she was still reaping the benefits.

Perhaps wisdom was simply an advantage of growing older, but she was a different person than the girl she had been, more secure in herself and what she wanted or didn't want. And because of this new self-knowledge, she recognized that James was destined to play a role in her life, and she had the honesty to acknowledge to herself that she wanted him to.

The difference in personalities between him and Dewi made it easy for her to accept what she felt for James, as she didn't feel she was comparing one to the other. One had been a storm, the other was like gentle rain. The intensity was different, but the result on a plant waiting to bloom was the same. The outpouring of water allowed it to thrive.

It was time. She had been dry for far too long.

"Shall we?" she asked once James had secured the horses to the tree.

"Yes."

He followed her to the edge of the water. She reddened when he spread the blanket in the spot he'd chosen the day he'd first taken her to the beach—and catapulted her straight to the stars. The look he threw her made it clear he had hoped to reawaken her memory. As if she could have forgotten such a thing.

"Are you going to dip your toes in again today?"

"Yes." Carys squared off to him. "And I want to go wade in the water this time."

There would be no hesitating. From now on she would live

her life to the full. After Dewi's death she had found solace in her role as mother and it had been enough to satisfy her, but now her daughters were grown and they didn't need her in the same way. Each had their own lives. It was time she thought of herself again. Last year she had left her country and started to build the second part of her life away from all she knew. It could have been scary, but it was actually freeing. If she wanted something, she could just take it, for who would stop her? No one. Hadn't she reflected only a moment ago that she was no longer the shy little girl she'd once been but a woman at ease with her needs and desires? It was one of the good things that came with age.

It brought you perspective, and the will to focus on what mattered.

If she wanted to take something, she *would* take it. She was not accountable to anyone.

"I will go in the water," she repeated, steeling herself. It would be as cold as last time, she supposed but no colder than the lake she was used to.

"You don't know how to swim." James sounded amused rather than trying to dissuade her.

"No. But you do. You will hold me."

"Will I?"

"Yes."

He didn't even blink. "Yes, I will."

They stripped down to their undershirts with the ease of long acquaintances, of people who had nothing to hide and were comfortable with one another. There was no embarrassment, no hint of teasing. There was nothing sexual in this disrobing. They were simply getting ready for a swim together. Well, a wade at the very least.

When they were ready, James held out his hand to her and gave a curt order, as was his wont. "Come."

She took his hand and followed him. They entered the water and walked steadily on until they were fully submerged. It was the only way to beat the cold. If they hesitated, they would not make it, and she did not want to be defeated on the first try.

Once the water reached to her shoulders Carys knew a moment of panic. This was very different from being in the tranquil waters of the lake by the village. James had crouched down to be at her level, and he was still holding her hands, for which she was glad because between the movement of the waves and the shifting of the sand under her feet, she was worried about going under. But with him holding her securely, she would be fine.

"Wouldn't you like to go farther out?" she asked none-theless. This could not hold much interest for him, who could make the most of the vast expanse stretching before him. "You could leave me here and go have a swim."

"No. I'm exactly where I want to be."

The answer was so perfect she sagged a little. Just then, a more forceful wave crashed against her, catching her on the chin. She let out a gasp when water sprayed her lips—and tongue. "Oh! But it's..."

"It's what?" James cocked a brow.

"The water..." She spluttered. "It tastes of salt! It's revolting!"

For a brief moment he stared at her, as if trying to make sense of what she had said, and then—then he burst out laughing. Carys looked on in amazement as he threw his head back and sent his deep, throaty laughter to the sky like an offering. James Mortimer was laughing. It was something she had never seen before and it was wonderful. It was thanks to her, which made it even more wonderful.

She wanted to pluck that delicious sound from his lips, and

swallow it. When the impulse became impossible to resist, she threw herself into his arms and kissed him.

After the initial shock, James lifted her into his arms to bring the kiss to a new level of passion, urging her to wrap her arms about his neck and her legs around his waist in support. Not worried about the strain imposed on him, knowing that in the water she would weigh next to nothing, Carys complied. It was a shocking position, there was no denying it. His hands were cradling her buttocks and with their undergarments wet and clinging to their skin, it felt almost as if they were naked. She could feel him, hot and hard, between her thighs.

His tongue licked, his teeth nipped, his lips caressed. The rest of him was not idle. His throat rippled with his grunts of pleasure, his stomach tensed and contracted every time he adjusted his footing on the sand, his hands kneaded her flesh.

It was perfect.

This man, this moment, this kiss was perfect. It tasted of salt, of desire, of joy. She knew then that when he came back from Margaret's village, they would address what was between them. And she knew they would be of one mind. People did not kiss like this unless they wanted to be together.

After a long moment, James let her go. His eyes were gleaming in the sunlight. A droplet of water had landed on his chin, just under his mouth, as if to taunt her. She licked it away and made a grimace. Too salty. She'd already forgotten.

James' lip curled at her reaction. "Forgive me for not telling you about the salt. I never thought to warn you."

Of course, he wouldn't have thought of mentioning some-thing so obvious to him, in the same way she wouldn't think of warning someone eating pottage that it was hot. "You're quite forgiven."

Would they have kissed if she'd known the water was salty? She couldn't be sure, since she had thrown herself at him in reaction to his laugh. And it had been the best, most heartfelt kiss she had shared with anyone since she'd lost her husband. It had been worth a mouthful of briny water.

"Will you wait for me, Carys?" James murmured against her temple. He was still cradling her in his arms and, despite the cold, she was loath to break the embrace.

"I will." Of course she would. "And in the meantime, I will learn to swim."

He smiled. "Just make sure not to come on your own. The sea can be quite treacherous, as you can imagine."

It warmed her that he didn't try to dissuade her, object to her being seen in a state of undress by another man or even simply forbid her to come, as many men she knew might do. Instead, he was encouraging her. "I'll be careful."

"I'll be looking forward to seeing your progress when I return. Now, come. Let's make the most of the sun to get you warmed up."

The following day at dawn, James left with Margaret. After her fit of madness of the other day, the woman seemed oddly subdued, willing to obey his instructions without comment. It was as if she had accepted she had lost him for good, and had no fight left in her.

One could only hope.

A small group of people had assembled in front of the barbican to bade them goodbye. James couldn't help a shudder. He didn't want to leave, not now, not when he could still taste the salt from the sea, mixed with Carys' sweetness, on his tongue.

After their kiss, he had taken her back to the blanket to dry and sat as far away from her as possible. Though sorely tempted, he had not dared do what he'd been aching to do and tumble her onto her back to devour her like he had the other day. This time she wouldn't have allowed him to get away with not reaching his own release, and he was still not ready for that. He needed to put his life and thoughts in order before he attempted to do what he had shied away from for so long. He already knew he would not find it an issue to perform with Carys, the way it had been with Joanne in the last few years of their marriage. His manhood definitely responded to her proximity, ignoring what his mind was telling him. His body was aching for the pleasure only a woman's softness could offer. His possession of her, when it came, would be complete.

Which meant he had to be sure he had mastered his fears before he attempted it, because it wouldn't be fair to her.

To his relief, she had not made any move to provoke him nor asked anything from him. She was giving him the time he needed.

"I will be as quick as I can, but it might be a month or more before I'm back." He did his best to address everyone, instead of staring at Carys. They had said their goodbyes the day before at the beach, in private. It had been the best way, as he didn't want to betray any emotion that would cause suspicion amongst the people at Sheridan Manor.

He knew she would be waiting for him, it was all that mattered.

"You take the time you need," Matthew told him, the same thing he'd told him when he'd left the year before. Aye, but so much had happened since then... Now he had more reasons than ever to want to hasten back home.

"Just make sure you're back to meet your grandchild in the summer. He will need all his grandparents by his side when the time comes," Branwen added, cradling her rounded stomach.

The new lady of the manor had started to show and had

never looked better. James smiled his thanks for her kind words, then stiffened when Margaret let out a scoff from behind him, unable to keep her venom in.

"Look at you holding yourself so proudly for doing nothing more than opening your legs and letting your husband rut on top of you, *my lady*." In her mouth the two words sounded like an insult. "I'll grant you that the man's more attractive than most, but you should—"

"Silence!"

James had never slapped a woman in his life, or even felt the urge to, but his fingers were itching something fierce right now. If she said anything else he would not be responsible for his actions. To think he'd believed her subdued!

Before he could say anything else, Carys planted herself in front of Margaret.

"Say one more word to my daughter and I will hit you. Hard," she hissed. "People with mangled jaws can't talk, can they? Nor can they use their mouths to rape unconscious men," she added, so low only he and Margaret heard. "Maybe I *should* hit you, and make sure no one else has to suffer because of you."

The smaller woman blanched, understanding that this was no idle threat, and he could not blame her. Every inch the protective mother, Carys was bristling with anger, and magnificent with it. James' body surged. Had they been alone, he would have swept her into his arms and kissed her until she couldn't breathe to express his admiration. As they weren't, he merely nodded at her.

Matthew stepped forward in turn, his face a mask of barely controlled fury. "Word of warning. If you ever dare show your face at Sheridan Manor ever again, *I* will personally deal with you. And I can guarantee you will regret ever bothering James, or talking to my wife the way you just did. Are we clear?"

There was such intent in his voice that Margaret took fright.

She turned to him with wide, pleading eyes. James glared back at her. How dare she suppose he would take her defense after all she'd done to him? Never had he come so close to hating anyone.

"Don't think for a moment I will help you," he said between his teeth. "If you don't want to travel home on your own, you will apologize to her ladyship immediately."

Margaret lowered her gaze to the ground and turned to face Branwen, "I'm sorry for talking about your husband rutting on top of you. I imagine it was nothing like that."

It was not the most gracious apology James had ever heard but he didn't have the will to insist. He just wanted to be on his way so as to return as quickly as possible.

"Would you rather I asked a guard to escort the woman back home?" Matthew asked, placing a hand on his shoulder in a gesture of support. "I can easily do that."

James was sorely tempted to wash his hands of the whole affair and accept the offer. Not only did he not want to leave Carys, but he couldn't wait to be rid of his sister-in-law. Then he thought of Joanne. Despite what Margaret had done, she was her sister. He owed it to his late wife to ensure her safety. That way he could come back home with a clear conscience and put everything behind him.

"No," he said, hoisting himself onto his horse before temptation overwhelmed him. He just had to do this. No one else would be able to convince Henry to take the woman on. "I thank you for the offer, but I will do my duty."

Chapter Eleven

At the end, it was close to two months before James could make it back to Sheridan Manor. Traveling with an unstable woman like Margaret had been even more taxing than he had anticipated. It took forever to talk her into getting back on the horse every time they stopped and she was not confident enough in the saddle for them to canter or even trot. Once, she had even fled during the night. As she had left on foot rather than stealing the horse she could barely control, it had been relatively easy to get her back, but still, that had meant another day's delay.

When they had finally reached her village, Henry had been nowhere to be found. His wife had informed them he'd gone to the fair in a town all the way on the coast and would likely not be back for another fortnight or so. Determined to impress upon his nephew by marriage the importance of not allowing his mother anywhere near Sheridan Manor again, James had elected to wait. Upon his return, as expected, the young man had been reluctant to agree it was his responsibility to look after his mother and it had taken James days he could ill afford to make him see reason.

Against all odds, it had been Henry's wife who had finally convinced him that they could take care of her. What had possessed the woman to agree to have such a mother-in-law under her roof, James could not fathom, but he had not wasted time wondering about her motivations, as it meant he was finally free to go.

All in all, it had been a nightmare and he'd sworn as he left that he would never set foot in that part of the world again.

His life was now at Sheridan Manor. He wanted no other. Work had been his refuge when he'd lost his wife and having Matthew had made him feel as if he'd not lost all the family he ever had. Now, with the promise of a baby coming, he felt more than ever that it was the place for him to be.

A baby—and a woman he wanted.

Carys, who had promised to wait for him.

As soon as he saw the dear, familiar shape of Sheridan Manor in the distance, he urged his mount into a canter, then into a full gallop. It felt good to have something to look forward to, and someone he wanted to be reunited with.

Matthew was the first person he saw when he brought his lathered horse to a halt in the bailey a moment later.

"James." The young man looked mighty relieved to see him. "You're back just in time."

In time for what? Heart beating hard, James jumped down from the saddle. The joy he'd felt coursing through his veins as his stallion's hooves had pounded the ground vanished in the blink of an eye. What did he mean? Surely Branwen's travails had not started yet? She was not supposed to give birth for another two months. Dear God, please, let there not be a problem with the babe. He knew all too well being born too early was a death sentence for a child. It had been for his first daughter.

"In time for what? Is it the baby?"

"No, thank God, Branwen is fine." A small smile, the same he always gave when talking about his wife, curved Matthew's lips. "But I was considering going to Wales and I didn't want to leave Sheridan Manor without a man I trust within the walls."

"You want to leave now?" James could hardly hide his surprise. With his wife so near her term, leaving should be the last thing Matthew was considering.

There was a sigh, proving he had not taken the decision lightly. "I know I should not even entertain the notion at this time, but I received a letter from Connor yesterday. After months of searching, he's finally captured Gruffydd ap Hywel, the rebel who almost killed him shortly after his marriage to Esyllt. He wants me to be there when he metes out his punishment, and I will admit it would please me also. The man has escaped retribution for far too long. It is time he paid for what he did to my brother's family, in good part through my fault."

James nodded. Now he understood Matthew's quandary, because he'd been told about the events of the past year. Indeed the Welshman deserved to die ten thousand deaths for what he had done, abducting an innocent child, then forcing her mother to hand over her husband so that the rebels could kill him in the most gruesome manner. The decisions Matthew had made at the time, before he'd come to trust his new sister-in-law, had cost Connor and Esyllt much suffering and months apart and he wanted to atone for it in every way he could. It was understandable.

But the moment was ill chosen.

"Are you going to go then?"

"Branwen is urging me to, even if she cannot travel herself. She wants to see her friend avenged as soon as possible and I feel I need to be there. But I would not have left while you were away. Now with you around, I know the place will be well guarded."

"Thank you." This proof of trust moved him so much he allowed himself to place a hand on the younger man's shoulder. "Go. I swear I will look after your wife."

And her mother.

Matthew nodded and ordered the groom to saddle his horse Raven, named for his wife, forthwith. "Go get a drink and something to eat," he told him next. "Forgive me for not joining you. I need to go see Branwen and say my goodbyes."

It was only early afternoon. Leaving without delay would ensure he was back in time for his child's birth. If he rode as if the demons of hell were in hot pursuit, he could be back within a fortnight. It was obvious that was what he intended to do.

After one last pat on his stallion's rump, James made his way to the room at the back of the solar. Before leaving, he'd deposited his personal set of keys in the iron chest and now that he was back, he felt naked without it. He was steward of the place, and he'd just been entrusted with the protection of its inhabitants by Matthew. He would not fail in his duty. Having restored the bundle to its rightful place at his hip, he turned around—and walked straight into Carys, who was coming through the door.

They almost collided and ended up locked in an embrace.

He couldn't help a smile at the irony of it. A year ago they had found themselves in that very room, two strangers unable to communicate. Now each was what the other needed and they understood one another all too well. Even better, they wanted the same thing. To be together.

"James," she said in a breathy voice. "You're back."

"Yes." Finally.

"It's been too long."

"Yes." Far too long. "Did you learn to swim in the end?"

He started when the inane question left his lips. Was that

all he could ask after so long apart from Carys? But she smiled as if he'd said the very thing she'd wanted to hear.

"I started to learn with Matthew, who took all three of us to the beach a few times. It was fine but then I decided to wait, because I want you to be the one to teach me."

His heart missed a beat when he realized he wanted that too. "Yes. I will show you."

Her smile wavered and she lifted her face up to him, as if readying herself for a confession. "I've missed you."

He didn't even blink. "Me too."

He had missed her every day, in little touches. Every time he'd seen a robin, he had thought back to her smile at the sight of the little bird, every time Henry's wife had taken her embroidery basket out, he'd compared her work to Carys' flowers and leaves, and found them lacking, every time someone had asked about his scar, he'd remembered the feel of her fingers on his skin.

Every time he'd lain in bed he'd ached for her.

Had it been that bad for her? Though he knew he shouldn't wish that agony on anyone, he found himself hoping it had. Because then it would mean she was as desperate for him as he was for her.

Right now she was looking at him with such intensity that, for a moment, he wondered if she would kiss him. Dare he take the first step if she didn't? He so dearly wished to feel her lips on his again. A light finger landed on his cheek before he could move or say anything. The brush on his skin sent shivers down his spine.

"I see your cut is healing nicely."

"Yes. Someone did an excellent job with the stitching," he said, his voice hoarse. "I'm told the scar barely shows."

"It doesn't." She sounded pleased that her efforts had been

rewarded. "You look as handsome as ever. Now, will you please kiss me?"

Oh, the wicked woman! To give him such an order in a matter of fact manner, when she had to suspect there was nothing he wanted more. James leaned in, blood roaring in his veins. Finally, the kiss he'd been desperate for. "I've thought of little else than kissing you during my—"

The door to the solar opened, interrupted his declaration. Whispers and muffled giggles heralded the arrival of a couple of lovers intent on making the most of a room they believed was empty.

James gritted his teeth. Not again! It was exactly like a year ago. They had gone full circle indeed. Who was it this time? Matthew, intent on making love to his wife one last time before going to Wales? Surely not. A wild tryst had been well and good then, but the comfort of a bed would be the best place the take a woman in her condition.

"Ah, Richard, please, be quick," Avice's voice, urgent amidst the rustling of clothes. Despite himself, James smiled. It would seem that the carpenter had not lost time in acting on his advice regarding the cook. During his absence, he'd gone to the woman, who'd only been too glad to surrender. Good for them. "I need to fill the pastries for tonight."

"Mm, don't worry, this will be quick. I, too, need to fill something."

James winced at the man's poor jest but, judging from the delighted chuckle that reached his ear, Avice was not put out in the least, used to her lover's dubious sense of humor. A grunt followed, then a moan. This was excruciating. When he finally dared look at Carys, who was still pressed against him, James saw that, far from being embarrassed this time, she was fighting a smile. His shoulders sagged in relief. Apparently, when it wasn't Matthew and Branwen she overheard, she saw the piquancy in the situation.

"Whatever shall we do?" she whispered, bringing her mouth to his ear.

For a moment he was tempted to answer that they should do exactly like the couple in the solar and make use of the table behind her to slake their own needs. Did she have any idea what it was doing to him to have her body so close to his?

"Get the hell out of here before it's too late," he whispered back. "I have no intention of hearing Richard make salacious jests about cream shooting out of him and I fear we are headed that way."

To his delight, Carys let out a tinkling laugh, far too loud for the purpose of staying discreet. When the couple in the other room became silent, he understood she'd done it on purpose to warn them they were not alone, just like he had done all these months ago with Matthew and Branwen by coughing. The grunts and moans were replaced by whimpers of dismay and grumbles of frustration. A moment later the door opened again, and silence settled back into the room.

"It seems that once again we were in the wrong place at the wrong moment," Carys murmured.

James could not quite agree. The wrong moment, yes, perhaps, but not the wrong place, since she was with him, and he was holding her.

"Yes," he said nonetheless. "Last time I couldn't even tell you what was going on. I felt really bad about that."

She giggled, a sound he had missed more than anything else. "There was no need for any explanation, I understood easily enough. And to tell you the truth, I'm glad I didn't understand what Matthew told my daughter."

Yes. It was probably for the best she had not heard what had been said.

He cleared his throat, guessing they would not kiss now. Somehow, because of the interruption, the moment had passed, and some sanity had come back to him. He now felt desperate to do what he'd wanted to do weeks ago. Kissing could wait, this confession could not. And perhaps with luck, it would lead to kissing—and more.

"Listen, Carys, the day Margaret arrived I had made up my mind to talk to you," he started, letting go of her soft, all too distracting body. If they touched, he might not be able to say what he had to say. "But after she'd claimed to be with child, I could not. I thought I would have to marry her and it did not feel right to open up in those circumstances."

Carys' face softened. "I understand. But you could do it now."

Yes. It was the obvious solution, but he was oddly intimidated. Where could he start? At the moment the revelation had struck him, maybe. It would have the added advantage of giving him the opportunity to apologize for his behavior.

"That day, when I saw Richard kissing you in the hall and offering you a future with him, I went mad."

"Yes. So I saw." The words could have sounded like a condemnation but the look in her eyes betrayed the fact that she had liked his reaction. Relief swept through him. He'd feared she would take him for a crazed, possessive madman laying his claim over a woman he had no right to. Apparently, she had not.

"I did not go mad because I thought you belonged to me," he specified nonetheless. "But seeing him kiss you and talk to you about the future made me see that I should have been the one to do it. Only... I didn't think I could."

"Why didn't you?" Carys' tone was encouraging. In that moment he knew she wouldn't judge. After what he had confided in her the day they had kissed, she would understand.

"Because I was scared. I still am." There it was. The truth

he had shied away from and thought he would have difficulty explaining, slipping out of his lips as naturally as if it had always meant to be uttered in front of her. "I'm scared of being with someone, of going through what I went through with Joanne, of losing more children. That is why in all the years since her death I never looked for anyone to be with. That is why I didn't dare examine what I have come to feel for you. I had resolved to end up my life alone and I didn't know how to question this decision, or even if I wanted to risk it." He shook his head. "Forgive me, I did not find the courage to accept what I wanted."

"There is nothing to forget. I understand."

Carys' chest constricted and expanded at the same time. Constricted because she was sorry for the pain James had been through, expanded because, despite his fears, all was not lost. It so happened that she might be the one person he could allow himself to be with.

It was time to make a confession of her own, a confession she had wanted to make for some time. She hoped it would give him the strength to act on his budding feelings for her.

"Perhaps with me you don't need to worry." She wrapped her arms around his waist, hiding her face against his chest. Not looking at him would help her to voice what she needed to say. She spoke with her mouth at his pectoral, willing him to give her a chance. "Because I will never give you children. There is nothing to fear. Whatever we do together, there will never be any issue. You will never father a child on me, I can—"

"You never know. You're younger than me, and my aunt was well past her fortieth year when she gave birth to her last son. My own mother had me late in life, as I told you."

He sounded almost offended that she should consider herself too old to be a mother, even though anyone in their right mind would concede that a woman her age was past her child-bearing years. But that was not what she meant.

It was obvious she would have to be clearer. She should have started with that part but she had hoped not to reawaken her own demons. "No. You don't understand. It's not just my age. I... I'm barren."

After saying the terrible word out loud, she nestled herself closer into his embrace and waited. There it was, the tragedy of her life. What would James do with the revelation? An arm, warm and comforting, wrapped around her shoulders.

"You are?"

She nodded, tears stinging her eyes. "The greatest regret of my life is never having known the joy of carrying my own children. I raised Branwen and Eirwen, and I love them dearly, as you know, but... it's not quite the same. It's not quite the same."

"No."

There was a silence. Then James asked, his voice low and soothing.

"How do you know you're the barren one? Forgive me for saying as much, but if your marriage never produced any children, it could have been due to your husband's inability, not yours. People are quick to put the blame on the woman in such instances, but as I see it, there are two people in a couple. Dewi could have been—"

She shook her head. He meant well, and she was grateful for it, but she knew the truth. As painful as it would be to bare it all, she would have to explain how she was certain she was unable to carry children. She could not afford to leave a shred of doubt lingering in James' mind, not when there was so much at stake. He needed to trust that he would never find himself in a position to father a child, or he would never give them a chance. Too scared of another potentially devastating loss, he would not be able to let himself go in her arms, no matter how much he wanted to, like he had with Joanne. Eventually, it would become a problem.

But they didn't have to go through any of this, not when she knew his seed would never take root inside her.

"No, I know I was the barren one, not Dewi," she said, her voice low and emotionless.

"How?"

Thank God he couldn't see her, for she had surely gone bright red. What would he make of her explanation, which would present her in an unfavorable light? But despite her embarrassment, she didn't consider lying.

"After Dewi's death, I was still quite young, at least young enough to hope I might bear a babe. I didn't want to remarry but I thought perhaps I could have a child or two of my own to love. As you say, I couldn't be certain I was the one at fault. If my husband had been the barren one then there was still a chance I could conceive with another man. So I..."

"You found yourself a lover," James supplied when she faltered. He didn't sound condemning, for which she was grateful. He made it seem like it had been a reasonable decision.

"Yes. It was not for pleasure, but because I hoped to get with child," she specified all the same. "Which was a good thing because it didn't... He wasn't..."

Once again, he came to her rescue when the words eluded her. "The man did not give you pleasure, you mean."

"No, not really."

Alun had not been rough, or even without skill, but she had never felt much in his arms. Certainly she had never experienced the storm of release Dewi had known to unleash inside her. Of course, he'd never noticed. Or perhaps he had, but he'd not really cared. And neither had she. Satisfaction had not been what their encounters were about. In her heart she had still been Dewi's wife, so perhaps the fault had not been all his. Perhaps she had her share of responsibility in the whole affair.

Perhaps she'd not been ready to accept another man's touch and let herself go. In any case, it did not matter.

What she had wanted from Alun, she'd never gotten.

"I bedded him for almost a year, to no avail. My womb never once quickened." Before he could point out that it did not mean anything, that sometimes it took time for couples to conceive, as evidenced by Branwen and Matthew, who could not keep their hands from one another and yet were still waiting for their first child to be born, she carried on. "One day a young woman came to the village, in search of Dewi. She said that he was her father and she looked too much like him for me to doubt her claim."

James' hold around her tightened. "Oh, Carys. That will have been terrible for you to hear." There was sorrow in his voice.

His concern warmed her. "No, it's not what you think. He was never unfaithful to me. Given her age, it was clear the girl had been conceived in his youth, before he and I met. But I understood that day that if he was her father, then he could not be the barren one in our marriage. I stopped seeing Alun after that and moved to the village close to Castell Esgyrn. There, I met Branwen and Eirwen. When their mother died, Branwen was ten and Eirwen not yet seven. I took them under my roof. Having them with me helped me make my peace with the fact that I would never have my own children."

"I'm so sorry."

"No, I'm the one who is sorry. I shouldn't complain to you, when you lost your children so tragically. 'Tis worse to lose someone you love and have seen grow than never to have had anyone."

He'd had to watch as his son slowly lost his grip on life. He'd had to accept he would never see his daughters open their eyes. He'd had to lift the lifeless body of his little boy from the cot he'd placed him in the night before, after a goodnight kiss.

All of this was worse.

"I don't know. Pain is pain, and you suffered, if for different reasons." He cupped her face in his hands. "I'm sorry, I wish you hadn't gone through that."

"Thank you."

"Is there anything I can do?"

"Yes. Hold me, just like that."

He did hold her. For a long moment in the small room, and then all through the night. Because when the time came to get to bed, he led her to his own room without a word. She lay next to him and then in his arms as if it were the most natural thing to do.

And perhaps it was.

Chapter Twelve

Waking up alone in James' bed, Carys took a long time to stretch and think.

How had the two of them ended up in a bed together and not made love last night? Every time they saw one another, sparks flew, and she knew they were equally desperate. Only the day before in the room at the back of the solar they had been on the brink of making use of the table, rickety as it was, exposed as it was. And yet, once they had been alone in a comfortable bed, away from prying ears and eyes, all they had thought about was hugging and offering one another comfort.

It could have been frustrating, yet somehow it had been more satisfying than if they had ripped at each other's clothes in a frenzy of lust, as they might have as untrained youths. It had seemed so much more meaningful.

Still, that didn't mean Carys had forgotten her need for James' touch, and she was sure he ached for her as well. There was no mistaking the way he looked at her.

That decided her.

Next time she saw him, she would drag him back to bed and make love to him. If he had accepted that he wanted to be with her, as she suspected, then he would allow himself to enjoy the physical pleasure she could bring him without worrying about the consequences. With Margaret out of the way, and the last of his doubts and fears mastered, they would finally be able to be together as lovers should be.

But once again, fate had other ideas.

As if it had decided that they would have to earn the right to be together by weathering all the setbacks a couple was capable of enduring, that morning, a boy came from the village to inform them that Eirwen had fallen ill with the measles.

The need to go to her daughter wiped everything else from Carys' mind. She stared at Branwen, who shared her dismay, then ran to the stables, where she asked for the gentle mare to be saddled.

"Oh, Mam," Branwen whimpered when she had caught up with her at last. Her great belly made her slower than usual, something she hated. "I wish I could go with—"

"No, you are not to place yourself or the babe in any danger, do you hear?" Her daughter could not fall ill as well, not when she was so near her term, not ever. What Matthew would say if he found his wife in bed with a fever when he came back from Wales was too dire to contemplate. How *she* would feel knowing she had not done what was needed to protect Branwen and her baby didn't bear thinking about. She would have to do this trip alone. "I will go to Eirwen, stay with her for as long as I have to. I won't come back to Sheridan Manor until she has recovered. Tell the people here no one is to visit me."

Tell James, especially, she wanted to add. He would want to bring her whatever comfort he could. But he was not to come anywhere near her, not when he could bring the illness back to the castle with him, not when he was barely recovering from a life-threatening fever himself. Carys had had the measles as a child, so she hoped she would not get it again, but even without this assurance, she would have gone to tend to her daughter. There was no choice. It was what mothers did.

Branwen nodded and placed a hand on her rounded stomach. "Tell Eirwen I love her and wish I had come. Tell her my son is impatient to meet his aunt."

"I will."

After one last kiss, Carys kicked her mare into a trot, wishing she had the skill to urge the animal into a gallop. But now was not the time to be reckless. If she broke her neck, it would not help anyone.

At the cottage, she found Mistress Ivy racked with guilt.

"I'm so sorry," she said, coming to hold the reins while Carys dismounted. "She insisted on helping with my neighbor Bessie's daughter, who fell ill three days ago. I should have insisted she stayed at home, but—"

"None of this is your fault." Carys forced herself to be reasonable, and say the right thing, but her chest felt hollow with worry. "Working with you has given Eirwen a purpose in life, I wouldn't want that taken away from her now. I know she would have wanted to help. And fortunately, you know all there is to know about the illness. If anyone can save her, it is you. Please take me to her."

Mistress Ivy tethered the horse to the fence and led her inside the cottage, where they found Eirwen sleeping on the pallet. Her face and neck were covered in red spots, her hair was matted with sweat and her breathing was much too fast. To combat the fever, she was dressed in only her shift. It was as bad as Carys had feared.

She fell to her knees and took her daughter's hand in hers. "*Cariad*. I'm here. It will be fine. I'm here."

There was no reaction.

"Don't let her lack of answer worry you." Her friend placed a hand on her shoulder. "The important thing is to keep her cool and make sure she drinks plenty."

"Yes. How long has she been like this?"

"It started yesterday. I didn't want to call for you straight away but when she was still the same this morning, I—"

"You did well. Now please, show me where you keep your supply of linen."

As she bathed her daughter's forehead later that night, Carys thought of James.

James, who had lost four children. James, who had fought for his life as well last year. James who had held her through the night, James who was afraid of his feelings for her. James, who was waiting at Sheridan Manor.

He needed to be told not to worry, that she would be back.

"Can I see your nephew again?" she asked Mistress Ivy in the morning, as she took the time to break her fast. She had not eaten anything the evening before and she was famished. "I need to send a message to Sheridan Manor."

"Of course. I'll ask Ellen to go get him. And then it's off to bed with you. You look half dead from exhaustion."

The day Carys and Eirwen finally came back from the village, James was not there to welcome them. He'd taken to helping the woodcutters fell the trees in the forest in a bid to stop obsessing about the fact that he'd once again been denied the chance to act on his desire for the woman he now felt able to be with.

She regularly sent him messages through the healer's nephew, assuring him all was as well as could be hoped with Eirwen. Her daughter was finally over the worst but still too feeble to be moved. In turn, he kept assuring her that all was well with Branwen, who was getting lovelier by the day and was now eager for her husband's return.

When he walked through the barbican one evening, exhausted by a whole day spent swinging his axe, he saw three women standing in the bailey. Three women talking in Welsh together, two with flowing dark hair and a blonde one dressed in a soft white gown. Someone he would have known anywhere.

At last.

His fatigue instantly forgotten, he joined them in a dozen swift strides.

"Carys. Welcome back." Was that his heart beating so loudly in his ears? It had to be, as he could see no one beating drums anywhere.

"Thank you. It's good to be back."

Unable to stop himself, he took her hand and squeezed it. He would have swept her into his arms and kissed her with all the strength of his relief but he could not, not in front of her daughters, who, he hoped, did not suspect what had blossomed between the two of them.

It was when he started thinking that they would have to be told, eventually, what he and their mother felt for one another that he realized the last of his doubts had vanished. Being away from Carys for more than a week had given him a taste of what life without her would be like and the prospect frightened him more than anything had for years. That was how he knew he was ready to act on his need to be with her.

Was it his imagination or had she lost weight? But of course she would have, too busy taking care of her daughter to think about herself. Would that he had been allowed to look after her these last few days! Well, perhaps from now on, he would be able to do just that.

Letting go of her hand, he turned to Eirwen. The girl looked rather more pale than usual, and she had lost some weight as well, but otherwise she appeared well enough. What a relief. He'd worried himself sick over her.

"It's so good to see you back on your feet. I hope you are feeling better."

"Thank you, I am." She smiled at him. "I'm glad to be back at Sheridan Manor."

He smiled back. Thanks to Mistress Ivy, her English had improved dramatically. She was also less shy and nervous than she had been a few months back. Not that she had ever been ill-at-ease with him, he was pleased to say. And he had always had a particular fondness for her. With her black hair, and dainty physique, she could be the daughter he and Joanne had never had.

Branwen took her sister by the hand and turned toward the main hall. "Come, I wanted to show you Rhwd's new trick. You'll love it, I'm sure."

What new trick? As far as James knew, the pup had not learned anything new in the last few days. If he hadn't known any better, he might have thought she wanted to give him and Carys some privacy.

He frowned. Had he been wrong? *Did* Matthew's wife suspect something had changed between him and her mother? She was quite sharp so she might well have. Did he mind? No. Let her think what she wanted, he was not ashamed of his feelings or his intentions.

"How is Eirwen, really?" he asked Carys as her daughters walked away arm in arm. Measles was a dangerous illness, which had claimed more lives than he cared to remember amongst his acquaintances.

"She'll be fine, she's stronger than you'd think from looking at her. But for a dreadful moment I thought I would lose her, and I couldn't bear it." She choked on a sob and then pressed a hand to her heart as if regretting her words. "Forgive me, James, I shouldn't have said that. You will know that horrible feeling, of course."

Unfortunately, yes, he did. But that did not mean she could not worry about her daughter. "There is nothing you cannot say in front of me, especially if it's something that's troubling you. I'll always listen."

A gleam appeared in her eyes. Relief? If he was not mistaken, there was something she wanted to tell him and she was only too glad to seize on the opportunity he was offering.

"As a matter of fact, there is something I need to tell you. The night before Eirwen fell ill, we slept together. I mean, in the same bed, in your room... I mean..."

He couldn't help a smile when she blushed the beautiful pink of the roses growing outside his window. Apparently, she could not be quite as bold as she would have liked. Because her shyness enchanted him, he decided to help her along.

"We did. And I think we were both hoping next time we would really *sleep* together."

The blush coloring her cheeks crept all the way to her temples but to his delight, she didn't shrink away from the honest answer. "I certainly am. But I'm sorry, I promised Eirwen I would sleep with her until she felt strong enough to go back to Avice's niece's bed. I hope you understand."

He did. After fearing she would lose her, Carys needed the reassurance of feeling her daughter was still here, next to her, alive and well. It was only natural. "Of course. You don't have to apologize."

They did not owe one another anything. He could wait. After all the delays they had endured, what was another few nights?

Torture, he decided, as he lay on his bed later that evening, stiff as a pike at the idea that Carys was back at Sheridan Manor, just yards away, warm in her bed, her body aching for his touch, and yet out of reach. The delay was bloody torture. He would have to do something about it. And he knew just what.

In the morning he entered the great hall with a new determination. If he and Carys could not spend their nights together, then they would have to make the most of their days. It was the perfect, obvious solution.

The only way not to die of frustration.

He found her sitting by the window, her embroidering basket on her lap. Her eyes opened as wide as if she had seen a ghost when he entered.

"You're wearing a green tunic."

James' lips curled into a smile at the unusual greeting. The woman always knew how to delight him. "Good morning to you, too."

The teasing had the desired effect. Carys blushed all the way to the roots of her hair. His smile widened. It was too easy to provoke a reaction out of her, and far too satisfying. Joy, embarrassment, desire. *Pleasure.* Yes. That was the one he wanted to provoke the most.

Dear God, he was losing it. He'd arrived in the room mere moments ago, and here he was, already thinking of ways to make her moan.

Which, if he were honest with himself, was exactly why he'd come.

"Good morning," she said, looking chastened. "I meant that I've only ever seen you wear black in all the months I've been here."

"That's because I usually wear black." He did, but for some reason, this morning he'd wanted to put on a tunic he hadn't worn in years. It was his only colored one and he realized only now that he was standing in front of Carys that she was responsible for the urge to take it out of the chest. "Whereas you always wear spring colors."

She glanced at herself as if she had not noticed it before. "Yes. I suppose I do."

"You most definitely do."

In fact, everything about her was vibrant. Today she was wearing his favorite light blue dress, the one that hugged her hips and swirled around her ankles every time she took a step. The effect could have been provocative had she not appeared so utterly unaware of the stirrings it caused in red blooded males. This was a woman at peace with her body, at the height of her beauty and confidence, not trying to rouse men's lust and all the more appealing for it.

The embroidery basket was placed back onto the floor. Carys stood up and walked over to him, causing her dress to dance around her in the way he liked.

"It took me a long time to fall asleep last night," she whispered once she had come to a halt in front of him. The words had his heart beating faster.

"What was wrong? Was it because of Eirwen?" Had her daughter's heath suffered a relapse?

"No." She placed a reassuring hand on his chest, just above where his thumping heart was. Could she feel it? Probably. "It was because of you. I cannot stop thinking about what you did to me on the beach that first day."

He groaned, not having expected her to be so outspoken. "Carys. Don't say things like that, or I might do it again."

"Is that supposed to frighten me?" She made a face he found adorable. How was that possible? His groin was on fire, and yet all he could do was think her adorable? It was odd to say the least. He should find her nothing other than breath-stoppingly arousing. "Well, it doesn't. As threats go, it is a very poor one.

Do you really think I would mind if you again did to me what you did then?"

"I think you might when I tell you it makes me want to do it *here*, in the middle of the great hall." His whole body surged at the thought of laying her on the table and feasting on her. To hell with everyone who might walk in, they would quickly understand they were not welcome and leave.

Carys sagged against him, clearly as aroused by the idea as he was. "James. Don't say things like that."

"Why not?" He wrapped an arm around her and drew her to him, making sure to let her feel how aroused he was. As it was all because of her, *for* her, it was only fair to let her know.

"Because it makes me want to push you on the floor and feast on *you*."

His heart skidded to a halt when she placed a hand over his hardness. Holy Mother of God. The woman was fearless. "Is that supposed to frighten me?" he rasped once he had found his voice again.

"I don't know. Does it?"

"Not in the least." Let her do whatever she wanted, feast all she wanted, however she wanted. The only concession to decency would be to take her to his room. No matter how strong his desire for her, he would *not* risk having one of her daughters, or both, walk in on her while she was using her mouth on a man. Having everyone see him pleasure her was one thing, allowing anyone to see her in such a compromising position quite another.

Yes. Taking her to his room was what he should do.

"I'm wearing the green tunic because of you," he said instead.

Carys blinked, as if not understanding what he meant. He wasn't sure he did either. And why in the name of God was he bringing this up now, when she had just hinted that she wanted to feast on him? When she was still pressing her palm against his hard length? He should have swept her into his arms and taken her up to his bed, so he could unfasten his hose and make the most of her offer before she could change her mind.

She spoke before he could. "Perhaps I should remove that green tunic."

"Don't you like it?"

"I do. But I don't think I can wait another moment to have you." He almost swallowed his tongue when she gave him a stroke, slow and deliberate, then another. Was she trying to unman him? Now was not the time to tease him so. His veins were burning, filled as they were with liquid fire. "So I'm thinking I should take you to my room."

Bless the woman. Her room was even closer than his. It was perfect. He groaned. "Yes."

"Master James?"

What the—

James could have howled in frustration. Instead he directed his anger at the man standing by the door. "Go to hell!"

"I'm sorry, I can't," came the hesitant answer, as if going to hell was a real option and Gilbert would have liked nothing more than to obey but could not. He looked ill at ease. Evidently, he'd guessed he'd interrupted a tryst. James stepped away from Carys, who had removed her hand from his groin.

"Well, what do you want?" He didn't turn around, for the blasted green tunic was shorter than his usual black ones and did not cover his raging erection.

"The king's nephew, the Earl of Lancaster is here. His lordship is still in Wales and Lady Branwen is resting. So it will be up to you to welcome him."

James and Carys stared at one another in stupefaction. The king's nephew was here at Sheridan Manor? Was fate so intent on keeping them apart that it invoked the King of England of all people? Were vindictive mobs of women, deranged sisters-in-law and life-threatening illnesses not enough? Were they to be interrupted, thwarted, denied at every turn? It looked like it.

He tugged at his hair in powerlessness.

Damn it all, he was going to have to welcome the man when all he wanted was to finally make Carys his.

Chapter Thirteen

Carys was still recovering from the shock of being told the King of England's nephew was here—and the frustration of being prevented to act on her desire for James—when Branwen entered the hall, her eyes blurry with sleep.

"I thought you were resting," Carys commented, walking over to her daughter. There were dark smudges under her eyes, proof that she did not sleep well at night. Of course, her growing belly would make her uncomfortable in bed, but Matthew's absence was probably responsible for her inability to sleep. In any case, whatever the reason for her fatigue was, she *should* be resting, not climbing up and down staircases.

"I was, but then I heard a commotion in the bailey and I thought I had better come see what it was."

Commotion. Yes, that was one word for it. How to announce what was happening? As two lowly born villagers, they were ill-equipped to receive such a high ranking noble and his retinue. Not to mention that, to Welsh women, the man was as close to an enemy as could be conceived. Branwen would understandably feel both out of her depth and resentful at the idea of having to welcome such a man, even if it was expected of her.

In the end, Carys just spoke calmly. "The Earl of Lancaster, the King of England's nephew, has just arrived."

"The—*who?*" Branwen fell onto the chair behind her.

"I know, I'm as stunned as you are."

Silence fell in the room. Nothing in the two women's former life had prepared them for such a moment.

"Oh, why did this have to happen while Matthew is in Wales?" Branwen moaned. "He would know what to do, but I cannot make conversation with the English king's nephew! I have no idea where to start."

Carys patted her hand in a comforting gesture. She didn't either. Fortunately, they had one weapon at their disposal. "Worry not. Once you have bade the earl welcome and offered his men refreshments, you will retire to your bedchamber on the pretext that your great belly is getting too much for you at this late stage." It would not even be a complete lie, anyone could see she needed calm and rest. "Just see him now, and James and I will take it from there."

Yes. James would know what to do, she was sure of it. Wasn't he with the retinue even now?

Branwen nodded. "Of course, you're right, as always."

"We will receive him here, rather than having you climb all the way up to the solar."

No sense in taxing her strength further. The man could take it or leave it. If he objected to being welcomed in the hall amidst the remnants of their morning meal, then he would just have to swallow his displeasure. Branwen's health was Carys' priority. She would ensure her daughter's comfort before pandering to a stranger's delicate sensibilities. The man might be nephew to the King of England, but he was nothing to her. Let him make what he would of the welcome they gave him. Matthew, if he ever got to hear of it, would side with them, she knew. Nothing would take precedence over his wife.

Carys opened the door and instructed William, the little page, to tell the steward her ladyship was up and ready to receive their prestigious guest.

James entered a moment later, followed by a man dressed in flamboyant clothes. He was just as tall as James, but slender and supple, in the way of youths who have yet to grown into their adult body. His blond hair was streaked with ginger strands, his eyes of a luminous brown. Carys supposed he could have been called attractive but somehow all she could think was that he reminded her of a weasel.

Branwen stood up and smiled a smile that didn't reach her eyes. She seemed to share her unfavorable first impression of the Earl of Lancaster. But perhaps they were both influenced by the fact that he was nephew to the man who had brought so much trouble to their country.

"My lord, you are right welcome at Sheridan Manor."

"I thank you."

The bow the earl gave was elegance personified. The kiss on the hand that followed, however, was more insistent than it should have been and Carys wondered for a moment if she had not seen his tongue touch Branwen's skin. Were these the manners at court? If so, she didn't care for them.

Before anyone could say anything, James was dismissed with a wave of the hand and a curt word. Though it was obvious he would have liked to stay, he could not ignore a direct order from such a man. Once the door closed, the earl gestured to Branwen that she should sit back down, a concession to her condition, in all probability, because he had the look of a man who liked to impress his status on others.

He didn't extend the same courtesy to her. It was clear she would have to stand and like it.

"If my men and I could rely on your hospitality, my dear Mistress Hunter, we would be most grateful." Despite the polite words, this was not a request. "The king, my uncle, is a day's ride behind us. He thought to call on Lord Sheridan on his way back from Scotland, where he won a resounding victory over the Scots at Falkirk and sent us ahead of the main retinue to ensure everything was made ready for his arrival."

Carys didn't have to look at her daughter to see how this arrogant speech would be received. Her own blood was boiling. The man was quickly making himself an enemy of them. He was taking pleasure in telling Branwen, who he knew to be Welsh, that his uncle had just crushed the Scots in the same way he had crushed her countrymen. Not only that, but he had made a point of calling her Mistress Hunter, as if to remind her, if she needed reminding, that she was neither noble herself nor married to a man who could lay claim to any title, his relationship with Lord Sheridan notwithstanding.

Weasel indeed, in more ways than one.

"You may, of course, rely on our hospitality for as long as you wish, but I'm afraid you will not get to see Lord Sheridan, or my husband, who is with him at present. Connor is in Wales, where he now resides, having found the country and its people much to his taste. I will be glad to tell your king when he comes that my brother-in-law fell deeply in love with the wife who was chosen for him. I'm sure he will be gratified to hear it."

A smile tugged at Carys' lips. Good for Branwen, who would not be intimidated and tell the pompous fool exactly where things stood. Wales and its people should not be dismissed so easily. There was more to them than met blind English eyes, he had better remember it.

"Mm." As could have been predicted, the earl was not chastened in the least. Entitled, noblemen like him were not easily made to feel at fault. "Are you telling me that an English knight of certain prestige can feel at home in a country of savages?"

"Lord Sheridan apparently can, and I'm sure you would agree he's a knight as worthy as they come."

"No doubt about that. I've met him on two occasions. He's a fierce warrior who's always been loyal to the crown. So I wager that what you took for contentment is only the satisfaction of knowing he is doing his duty to king and country. Or... perhaps I'm wrong and Welsh women are capable of turning a man's mind completely. Do you know, now that I've seen you, I can well believe that might be the case." His voice became thick as boiled honey, and just as sickly. "Your accent is quite delicious, Mistress Hunter. As is the rest of you."

From where she was, Carys couldn't see the earl's face but she didn't miss the stiffening in Branwen's body. It was not difficult to guess he would be eyeing her up with undisguised lust. She took a step forward, reminding him he was not alone with his host. He seemed to have quite forgotten it.

But instead of reverting to a more seemly behavior, when he heard her move, the earl waved her away like a bothersome fly. "You can leave us," he snapped without even looking in her direction.

The look of panic flashing through Branwen's eyes at the command lit a matching fear in Carys' chest. The earl was dismissing her, with the obvious intent of seducing the lady of the castle while her husband was away. It was staggeringly bold of him but she could not claim to being surprised. English noblemen seemed to think women of lesser rank, and Welsh women in particular, were theirs for the taking. Nothing protected Branwen. Not the fact that she was married, or with child. All the Earl of Lancaster knew was that she was here, she was beautiful, and he was aroused. With her husband away, he thought nothing or no one could stop him from taking what he wanted.

Well, Carys would try if it killed her. She would have done so for any woman, but this was her daughter. She would not give up so easily.

"My lord, I think I hear horses passing through the gate. Perhaps it is the rest of your retinue?" she said in an attempt to make him see he had better not think of doing what he had in mind. "Or the king himself, having made good time?"

"I hear nothing. But by all means, go and see for yourself. We don't need you here."

"I will—"

"Just leave, woman!" With that command he finally turned to look at her. His eyes were swirling with ill-contained irritation. It was clear he was trying to suppress a show of temper not for her benefit, but so as not to scare Branwen, whom he intended to seduce into surrender. "Mistress Hunter was about to show me Welsh hospitality. I think it is high time I see for myself what it is about Welsh women that pleases men as discerning as Lord Sheridan."

As he obviously took her for a servant, there was nothing she could do. Even if she revealed who she truly was, namely his host's mother, it would not matter one bit. Someone like her, though not exactly a menial, was of no consequence to an earl. As a noble, he outranked her ten times over. As an English subject, he was her superior in every way. As a man, he could dispose of her with a flick of his wrist.

She had no choice but to leave and find someone who could actually stop him. If not a noble, at least a strong, English man who could physically restrain him. Because there was no way she would allow anyone to rape her daughter, be he the nephew of the King of England.

"I'll go and get help," she told Branwen in Welsh, certain the man did not speak the language. "I promise you won't have to—"

"Will you just cease your blabbering and leave, before I have you whipped for your insolence!"

"Go," Branwen instructed her softly. She looked about to faint but determined to protect her from the man's ire.

Heart in her throat, Carys flew out of the door. James. She had to get James. Somehow, between them, they had to stop the lecher. They could worry about the consequences later. The important thing was to save Branwen from assault. How long would the earl countenance her refusal to be wooed? Not long, in all probability. And when he saw he would never be able to charm an agreement out of her, he would simply take what he wanted by force.

As she drew near the barbican, she saw a horse thunder through the gate, his reckless pace betraying the impatience of the rider. It did not take her long to identify him. Matthew! Back from Wales at the most opportune moment. Finally, fate seemed to be on her side.

Relieved beyond measure, Carys ran up to him. "My l—"

"What is it?" he asked before she could finish the word. Obviously her anguish was all too glaring. He jumped down from his horse and took her hands in his. His face was a mask of worry. "Is it the babe? Branwen? Where is she? Am I too late?"

"The baby is fine," she reassured him, while James drew near. He, too, it seemed, had picked up on her agitation. Not that it was difficult, she imagined. She could feel herself tremble. "She's in the great hall, with the king's nephew, the Earl of Lancaster. He arrived earlier that morning."

Matthew's shoulders relaxed and she hated having to renew his fears. Because although there was no problem with the baby,

Branwen was most definitely in danger, and she needed help. Carys exchanged a glance with James, who instantly tensed up. He'd understood what the issue was, then... Perhaps, like her, he'd been unsettled by the kiss on the hand earlier, or perhaps he'd heard unsavory stories about the earl while talking to the men in his retinue. It mattered not how he'd guessed what was going on. He knew, that was the important thing. She wouldn't have to impress him with the urgency of the situation.

"I stayed with them at first but then he sent me away. I fear his intent, he was looking at her with—"

Before she could say anything else, Matthew let out a roar and turned toward the main hall, murder in his eyes. He didn't have time to take more than one step, however. James had placed himself in front of him, as solid as a wall.

"You stay right where you are, my boy."

The shocking familiarity didn't even register on Matthew's face. He grabbed James by the tunic, drawing him so close their noses touched. "You don't understand! I have to go to Branwen, I cannot have her alone with a man intent on... She cannot go through that again! Not again, do you hear! I married her, I promised to keep her safe. Let me go, I need to stop the bastard before he—"

For all his determination and muscular physique, Matthew's efforts at trying to push past James were in vain. The man was immovable. Carys shivered. She had never before noticed how strong he was and the realization made her quiver.

"No! If you go you'll rip him to shreds. I'm not saying he doesn't deserve it, but then you'll get executed for killing the king's nephew," he said in growl. "What of your wife then? Your child? You cannot die, Branwen needs her husband and the babe needs his father. So *I*'ll go. And I'll stop him, I swear." Before he went he threw a glance at her, one that burned a path all the way to her soul. "For the love of God, Carys, make him see that I'm right."

With those words, he flew toward the great hall.

Carys' heart lurched to a stop. He *was* right, damn him. If Matthew entered that room, he would prevent his wife's rape. That was not in doubt. Anyone trying to hurt Branwen wouldn't stand a chance against a man as strong and irate as he was. The earl would be stopped. But the problem was, Matthew would not leave it at that. He would not be able to stop himself from making the earl pay for all the other men who had assaulted Branwen over the years. By the time he had finished with him, there would be nothing left of the King of England's precious nephew.

And tomorrow, when Edward arrived, there would be retribution. It didn't bear thinking about. Her daughter would never survive the loss of her husband.

Carys lifted pleading eyes to Matthew, knowing that if he decided he could not stand idle while his wife was in danger, she would not have the strength to restrain him physically. She needed to appeal to his reason.

"Just wait a moment before going in. James will stop the earl. He promised he would and I trust him. He's right, it's the best solution."

"This is all my fault. I should never have left!" The pain, the powerlessness etched on his face was enough to tear at Carys' heart. His beloved wife was being assaulted and he could not help her, in the same way she could not help her daughter. It was an awful sensation and she could only sympathize with him. "You know what she suffered... You know why I cannot bear to—"

"I do. I'm her mother." Indeed she knew about her daughter's traumatic past. She had hoped that now that Branwen was happily married, they would be able to put it all behind them. Apparently, it was not that easy. "But I also know she would beg me to stop you from getting into that room. You need to let James do this, however hard it is, because she would die without you."

"Of course." Despite the agreement, he sounded less than convinced.

It was only then that the reality of the situation hit Carys.

When the English king arrived, *James* would be the one facing royal retribution.

～

Sitting in the damp, stinky cell, James was cradling his head in his hands.

This had been a disaster. He had feared all along it would end badly for him, but there had been no other choice. Someone had to stop the earl from raping Branwen, and that someone could not be Matthew. No matter what, James would not allow a man who was about to become a father to put himself in danger.

There was, of course, another reason for his intervention.

Guilt.

He had promised Matthew he would safeguard his wife before he went to Wales, and he had failed. The least he could do now was make sure no one but him suffered the consequences of his inability to protect the woman Matthew loved and their child.

When James had burst into the hall, he'd found the earl bent over a deathly pale Branwen. Her bodice had been ripped open and her hands, wrapped around her swollen stomach in a protective gesture, were shaking. The vile man was fumbling at his hose, his intent all too clear.

"You bastard!" James said between his teeth, before rushing over to her. Thankfully, he'd arrived in time, though not early enough to spare Branwen a fright.

She let out a gasp when she saw him. "James. *Diolch.*"

As soon as the words had left her mouth, she fainted. It was as if after having done her best to hold on to her sanity while she was alone, she was finally allowing the full horror of what was happening to overwhelm her. James could barely imagine what Matthew would have done if he had been the one walking in on the appalling scene. If he, who was not in love with Branwen, had felt his blood shoot straight to his head, her husband would have gone mad.

He fell on the younger man like a rabid dog on its victim. The earl deserved to be torn to shreds for what he'd wanted to do. How dare he assault a woman, and a woman who was married, heavy with child and nearing her term! Had his men not chosen this moment to come get him, he might well be dead right now.

As it was, the king's nephew had been saved in extremis. Alone against six men, James had had no choice but to surrender.

Once he'd regained the ability to talk, the earl had ordered his attacker be taken to the dungeon, for the king to deal with on the morrow. Matthew, who had rushed into the hall along with the royal guards and run straight to Branwen, had been unable to do anything to prevent his arrest. Too bruised to stand on his own two feet after the beating he'd received, James had been carried to the dank cell where he'd spent the remainder of the day and the whole night pondering what his punishment would be.

Death, obviously.

One did not try to throttle a member of the royal family and live to tell the tale. One was made an example. The only thing he didn't know was *how* he would die. In all probability, it would be both gruesome to watch and excruciating to endure.

Heaven help him, but he didn't know how he was going to bear it.

The trap door above him creaked open, the sound ominous in the darkness.

His whole body tensed up in dread. Was it dawn yet? Or had the earl and his men decided to come and amuse themselves with him before his execution? They had ruled that the king would be the one to decide his fate but no one had specified that the prisoner should be in a state to hear the judgment pronounced. He could well end up being brought in front of Edward still breathing, but wishing to be dead already.

The yellow light of a torch filled the dark hole above him, then the ladder was lowered down. James screwed his eyes shut, in a vain attempt at keeping calm. The mysterious visitors were actually coming down, which meant they were not going to be satisfied with simply shouting taunts from above. Shackled as he was, weakened by the earlier beating, he would be unable to defend himself. Well, at least he would not give them the pleasure of knowing that he dreaded what was in store for him.

The wood groaned when the first tormentor started to descend the ladder. How many were there? There was no noise coming from the room above, no scuffling of boots, so perhaps the man was alone. He waited, knowing he would find out soon enough who had come to make him regret attacking the prestigious Earl of Lancaster. But the person standing in front of him when he finally dared to open his eyes was the last one he'd expected to see.

Carys?

Was he dreaming? He'd been in that cell practically all day and most of the night. As a result, he was chilled to the bone, thirsty and slightly delirious. Was he imagining the woman he most dearly wanted to see? It was all too possible.

"What are you doing in the dungeon?" he croaked, hoping she was really here. He'd so dreaded dying without being able to speak to her one last time.

"I've come to take you out."

Chapter Fourteen

J ames blinked. He was not dreaming then. Carys was truly here in front of him, she was not a vision. Visions did not talk, they didn't smell like fresh air, and they did not cradle men's faces in their soft hands.

He leaned into the caress, then turned his head to place a kiss on her palm. The need to rub his cheek against her was so strong he didn't even try to resist. Only moments ago he had been drowning in fear and despair and Carys was offering him a respite from the horror he was facing, short as it may be. He'd been right all those months ago. Miracles did happen. And against all odds, one had come to Sheridan Manor for him. The only problem was... It had come too late. He would never get to reap the benefit from it now.

In the morning he would be dead.

Mm. Best to put that idea out of his head and ask what he needed to know instead.

"How is Branwen?" He had tortured himself all day over the memory of her, lying pale and limp, in her husband's arms. Had the shock of the assault caused her to go into premature labor? It would not be unheard of. Had she lost the babe? He prayed it was not the case.

"She's fine. Thanks to you." Carys' voice wobbled. "You saved her, like you said you would, you arrived in time. Oh, James, I can never thank you enough for what you did."

"Please." He shook his head. There was no need to thank him. "What else could I have done? I don't regret it, even if I have to—"

"You're not going to die for it!" There was such fierceness, such conviction in her voice that James stared. How could she make such promises to a condemned man? "Didn't you hear what I said? I'm here to take you out of this cell."

There it was again, the shocking declaration. Earlier, lost to the joy of seeing her in front of him, soft and real, he had not really paid attention to her words, because he knew she would never be able to get him out of this hellhole. She seemed convinced opening the trap door and getting the ladder down was all she needed to do to free him. It was not.

"You can't get me out." He gestured at the shackles holding him captive. Evidently she had not imagined he would be tied up and chained to the wall when she had hatched her mad plan, but it was time she faced the truth. "How did you get in here anyway?"

"Through the trap door."

The woman had the gall to give him a slanted smile, as if the answer to his question was obvious. It was, since the trap door was the only way to access the dungeon. But of course he was not wondering if she had slipped through the cracks in the wood like some sort of magical rain. Rather, he couldn't understand how she had not been seen—and stopped—by the guard stationed in the room above the dungeon. How had she convinced him to let her through? Had she appealed to his sensibilities, claiming she wanted to see the condemned prisoner one last time? Against all odds, the man might have taken pity on her. She was irresistible, James knew it all too well.

And now that she had gained access to him, she thought she could get him out. But it was no use. Tied to a hook on the wall by an iron chain, he was not going anywhere, even if the door was open.

Carys straightened up, determination etched all over her face. "Let's go. I should think you've spent enough time in that vile place. I certainly have."

"We cannot go," he repeated, getting worried by her refusal to accept facts. Had her mind been unhinged by his arrest? By now she should have seen it was hopeless. Even if she had secreted a weapon about her person, she would never have the strength to break the chain or the time to saw through it before the guard called her back. "How do you suppose to free me of my shackles?"

"With the key the Earl of Lancaster gave me."

James stared at her. The earl, the man who wanted him dead, had given her the means to set him free?

"What do you mean? Why on earth would he do that?"

It didn't make any sense. The man meant to keep him prisoner until the king arrived. He would have known she would try to free him if she were allowed into the dungeon. So had he thought to amuse himself by giving her false hope? Had the guard outside been asked to let her through, and reinforcements called to prevent an escape? His confusion must have shown on his face because Carys explained, her voice as steady as if they were having a discussion in the peaceful solar instead of a stinky dungeon.

"I left him no choice. Did you really think I would give up and leave you to rot while waiting for your execution?" She gave something like a snort, as if the notion was too ludicrous to contemplate. "Matthew did all he could to get you freed. In vain. So I went to the earl's bedchamber once everyone had gone to bed."

Everything within James dissolved. He could think of only one reason she would have done this. To bargain for his life. And there was only one way she could have succeeded. By using her body. She had gone to a man she knew full well was not above raping women even when they were married and with child, and done what was required to earn a pardon. She had sold her body for him.

It could not be borne.

He could not live with that burden on his shoulders, with the knowledge of what Carys had sacrificed for him. How had she not guessed he would rather die than allow her to be harmed in any way?

"Please tell me you're lying."

"I'm not."

As if to prove it, she knelt in front of him and extracted a small key from her bodice. He recoiled when she made to insert it into the lock holding his shackles.

"No!"

There was such anguish in that one word that Carys paused. Setting James free would have to wait. Right now, he needed reassurance more than he needed his freedom. He seemed to think she had bought a pardon with her body, a reasonable assumption given the circumstances, she had to admit. That had not been her intention, but deep down she knew she would have done whatever the earl requested to save the man she loved, including sleeping with him. Because she simply could not let James die now.

No price would have been too high to pay.

But James did not seem to share this opinion. Before anything else, before she attempted to free him, he needed to hear she had not been raped. So she looked at him straight in the eye and said what he wanted to hear.

"The vile man didn't touch me, I swear. I didn't use my body to free you." She infused all the conviction she was capable of in her words. He needed to be left in no doubt about it; they could not have this hanging over them for the rest of their lives. "You can accept your freedom without guilt. I was not hurt in any way."

Everything within him seemed to relax and after a moment, he held out his hands to her, finally allowing her to use the key to unlock the shackles.

"What happened then?"

As she went to work, Carys began to relay what had happened in the earl's bedchamber earlier that night.

When she had entered, she'd found the man sound asleep, as she'd hoped, lying flat on his stomach. Even better, his clothes were heaped haphazardly on a chair next to the bed. Moved by instinct, she snatched the undershirt from the top of the pile and hid it under her cloak. It could only aid her in her plan to be in possession of such an incriminating item.

Then she cleared her throat and, heart thumping hard in her chest, waited for him to wake up. It didn't take long. When he saw her standing at the foot of the bed, the earl opened wide, incredulous eyes. A quick look around the room told him she had come alone and his lips curved into a slow smile.

"Come for a fuck with a member of the royal family, have you, wench?" He scoffed and she realized he had not even recognized her for the woman who had been in the hall with Branwen that morning. It was hardly surprising, as he had barely spared her a glance. This might work to her advantage, so she didn't rectify the mistake. "You wouldn't be the first one, believe me, but you're wasting your time. Be gone with you. I don't bed women who are old enough to be my mother."

"I may be old enough to have birthed you but I count myself lucky that I did not," Carys answered calmly. Let him insult her all he liked, she cared not. "It is not hard to guess your poor mother must be ashamed of the man you have become."

For a moment he just stared, as if stunned by her declaration. In that moment, with his hair ruffled and his naked, slightly hollow chest, he appeared little more than a youth. By her estimation, he could not be much older than twenty summers. How could someone so young be so evil, she wondered? Anger boiled anew. Because he was English, and high born, he felt he could use people the way it suited him. Well, it was time he learned actions had consequences.

"How dare you speak to me thus?" he demanded, his body tensing. He was not used to being questioned and he didn't like it one little bit.

"I dare because *you* dared attack my daughter and have condemned the man I love to death. And now I have no other choice but to avenge the one and save the other."

"Save?" Another scoff. "You think you can save the miserable man's hide by offering yourself to me in reward for my generosity? I'm sorry but I am not tempted, as you can see. Your dubious charms fail to rouse my blood."

In a flamboyant gesture he threw aside the covers and stood next to the bed. Carys saw that he was stark naked and, just as he'd said, limp as a worm. She could not repress a sigh of relief at the sight. There had always been the danger of him pouncing on her, not through real desire, of course, but just to show her her place. It was clear, however, that he had no intention of tumbling her into bed.

"I'm relieved to see you feel no desire for me, because I certainly feel none for you," was her answer. "I am not here to offer my 'dubious charms', whatever you may think."

"How do you suppose to force me to release the steward

then? My mind is quite made up. He tried to kill me. He will pay for it."

This was it. The moment of truth. All day, while Matthew had done his best to talk his way out of the situation, Carys had agonized about the best way to pressure the earl into releasing James. Finally, after much deliberation, she thought she might have come up with the solution. The man's weakness needed to be used against him, and she had a fair idea of what that might be.

She took in a deep inhale, praying she was right.

"Tell me, what do you think the king will think when he is told tomorrow that his nephew boasts about his superiority over him to anyone who cares to listen? When he hears the Earl of Lancaster thinks himself a better lover than his liege and is not above ridiculing his uncle for his exploits in bed?"

The man's eyes widened. "When have I ever done that, pray?"

"Just before you pounced on my daughter Branwen this morning," Carys hissed, her wrath igniting a fire within her. In that moment she felt invincible. "You said you would show her what a real man can do, as opposed to a cripple in his late fifties. I recall every word, as does she."

"I never said—"

"Branwen will swear that you raped her, her husband will attest to it as well. I will tell the king I saw and heard it all, Master Mortimer and everyone at the castle will confirm the story. Faced with such overwhelming evidence, he will not be able to doubt the veracity of the claim."

She knew she was putting herself at risk by provoking the earl, but thoughts of James rotting in his cell gave her the courage she needed. As horrid as it was to imagine him in the dank place, all alone and dreading the arrival of dawn, it was nothing compared to the fate awaiting him. She had no illusion about what the English king would do. A man capable of subduing the Welsh and the Scots would not hesitate in punishing someone who had attacked a member of his family and almost killed him. Edward would be merciless.

But she would too.

She would do what it took to protect her family and the people she loved.

"Is it really worth taking the risk of such a tale reaching the king's ears, my lord? Only you can tell. But I would think very carefully if I were you, because your uncle will have little choice but to heed Branwen's words when she stakes her claim, supported by her husband, brother to one of his most loyal knights. Are you so confident he will not believe her when she says you wanted to show her how much more manly than the king himself you were?"

"He would have to believe I raped her first!"

Carys didn't let that bother her. Unfortunately, a man who acted the way he had acted toward her daughter could not be new to the crime. No, she could well imagine the charge of rape had been laid at the earl's door before. The real question was not whether Edward would believe it, but whether he would think it worthy of punishment. From what she'd heard, he was not exactly the scrupulous sort himself when it came to women.

Feeling sick to her soul at the depravity of men, she straightened her spine.

"He will have no choice but to believe her, because she has everything she needs to back her claim." Thanks to her, Branwen would be in possession of the earl's undershirt, which they would make sure to tear and bloody before it was presented to the king. "The garment you discarded before pouncing on her, for one."

She glanced to the pile of clothes meaningfully. But, far from being worried at the realization that his undershirt was missing, the earl scoffed. "A man doesn't need to get naked to take his pleasure with a woman. Are you still a virgin that you do not know this, old crone?"

"Perhaps the shirt alone will not be enough," she conceded, not allowing the insult to rankle her. "But that will not be her only proof." Carys smiled grimly when she remembered Margaret using her knowledge of James' body to make him believe they had slept together. It had been what had made him take her claim seriously. Despicable as it was, it was worth using the same weapon. She arched a brow and nodded in the direction of the earl's groin. "How would she know how small your appendage is if you had not raped her? Or are you telling me it is common knowledge at court?"

Fury exploded in the man's eyes. Had it been wise to add that last provocation? Probably not. But she had not been able to resist, knowing that someone like him would hate to be mocked in his virility. One had to strike where it hurt, and she did not have any sword. More's the pity. Then she would have been able to punish him the way she wanted, and make sure he did not assault anyone else ever again. He snatched the sheet to cover his offended manhood when she'd feared he would launch himself at her in retaliation.

It was then Carys understood that she had won.

It seemed that, against all odds, the man had some vestige of honor left. If he had not, he would just have killed her for her slight. Of course, the fact that he hadn't struck her might not have anything to with honor. She had claimed everyone at Sheridan Manor was in accord as to what version of events to present to the king when he arrived. With her out of the way, they would still present their grievances, and add her murder to the list. He was cornered and he knew it.

"You would lie and blackmail me?" he rasped once he was covered.

There was no hesitation. She would have done far worse for Branwen and James and he was a fool to even doubt it.

"Yes, because they are the only weapons I have. Were I a knight instead of an untrained woman, believe me, I would silence you in a more permanent way for raping my daughter."

"Wait, I didn't—"

"Only because someone stronger stopped you before you could," she spat, unable to believe he thought the fact that he had been prevented from actually raping his victim would be an argument in his favor. "And you had every intention of doing so. You frightened her out of her wits, which is bad enough, and her being with child and so close to her term! She fainted from sheer terror because of what you did. Or did you not see that?" For a moment Branwen would have thought herself back to her old life, before Matthew, when men thought they could dispose of her body. It was unbearable. "You nearly sent her husband mad with anguish. You put her babe in danger. What you did is unforgivable. Believe me, if I had James Mortimer's strength, you would be dead by now."

Carys had thought herself powerless but, in that moment, she saw that he believed her. The mighty Earl of Lancaster, nephew to the King of England, thought her a force to be reckoned with.

She pressed her advantage.

"So now the choice is yours: either you kill an innocent man, someone so below your notice you won't even derive any satisfaction from his murder, or you risk the ire of your uncle, who happens to be the most powerful man in all England, Scotland and Wales, a man who subjugated two proud nations and created a whole dynasty." God knew she hated the man, but if ever there was a time to list King Edward's achievements, this was it. "How do you think he will take the humiliation of being told in front of his men that you think him unable to perform in bed? Do you think he will really give you the benefit of the doubt?"

Here she was relying on the fact that the young pup had already roused his uncle's hackles with his arrogance. For all she knew, the two men trusted one another implicitly. Heart beating, she waited. It quickly became obvious, however, that she had been right to gamble on him having riled the king in the past. The earl's face became a stony mask, as if he knew he would not so easily talk himself out of the hole she had dug for him.

Finally, he uttered the words she had been hoping to hear. "What do you want?"

"My daughter will be excused from seeing the king when he arrives. She will plead an indisposition, on account of her being with child." Her voice was as hard as steel, betraying her determination. But she would not have Branwen setting eyes on her aggressor ever again or meeting the equally lecherous Edward. Matthew would have to welcome him, of course, and he might well want to air his grievances about the man's nephew once he was in front of him, but she was confident she could talk some sense into him before the confrontation.

"Agreed." The earl saw the benefit in this for him and sounded only too glad to grant her this wish. If Branwen didn't see the king, she would not be able to accuse him of having raped her.

"And, secondly, you will release James Mortimer. Now. Tonight. He will leave the castle before dawn, you have my word on it, and not come back until the royal retinue has left. With him gone, and Branwen safely tucked away in her bedchamber, no one will breathe a word of what happened to the king during his stay at Sheridan Manor. You will be safe."

The young man stared at her a long moment, weighing her

determination. She stared right back, unblinking. Never had she felt more ready to stand her ground.

"Eventually, he surrendered," Carys told James, who had watched her with wide eyes during her whole story. "I left the room in possession of the key that would free you, and his promise no one would stop me from entering or exiting the dungeon."

"So you saved my life?" His voice was full of awe.

"There was no reason for you to be killed in the first place, so it is little achievement," she retorted promptly. Why should he be punished for doing no more than defend an innocent woman from rape? He had done nothing wrong.

"I beg to differ. You are one amazing woman, Carys."

"I don't know about that." But she felt amazing, and other things besides, when she was with him.

They were now standing in front of one another, their bodies almost touching. Carys wanted to throw herself against James' chest and melt into his arms but he seemed strangely reluctant to hold her.

Her heart broke. She had been so certain they could finally be together now that he was assured to live!

"Why aren't you taking me in your arms?" she whispered when it became impossible to ignore the need to feel that he was here, safe, alive. "What does a woman have to do to earn a kiss from you? I would have thought that saving your sorry hide might be enough, but apparently it—"

He stopped her with a finger on her cheek.

"Carys, please. I..." He gestured at himself, at his blood-crusted clothes, his jaw covered with a black shadow, his filthy hands. "I would like nothing more than to kiss you right now but I cannot. Look at me."

"I *am* looking at you. And I want you to kiss me, so desperately. I don't care about the blood, or the dirt, except for wishing you had never endured all you had to endure," she finished in a sob. "I thought for a moment that I would lose you, and it almost—"

This time he stopped her with the fiercest kiss she had ever received, hot, decadent, utterly delicious. The kiss she had dreamed about for weeks.

"James." She ground herself against him and had the satisfaction of feeling him hard against her stomach. Say what he might about the state of him, she could have made love to him right here, right now, just to prove to herself that she had succeeded in her mission. But unfortunately, it wasn't an option. "No, we can't," she forced herself to say.

"Of course, we can't," he said in between feverish kisses. "Not here, in a filthy dungeon. Not now, when I smell worse than the castle midden. When I do take you, it will be in my feathered bed, not on moldy straw. When I cover your body with mine, I will be clean, not covered in God knows what filth. When I hear your moans of pleasure, I will enjoy them without having to worry about who might hear us."

Oh, was he trying to make her mad, talking about what he intended to do while saying they could not lie together?

"I mean that you have to leave," she said against his lips. She had promised the earl that James would not see the king, but that was not the reason why she needed him out of Sheridan Manor. She didn't trust the man as far as she could spit and would take her own precautions. "Dawn is nearing and the king is due to arrive today. You need to be out of the way when he does, in case one of the earl's men goes to him to tell him that you almost killed his nephew. I cannot risk having you captured again. You won't escape retribution a second time."

He stilled against her. "Yes. You're right."

"Hide in the village. We will send word to you when the

king's retinue is gone and you can safely come back. Now, let's go. I don't want to be caught because we lingered too long."

"No."

After one last kiss, he followed her to the wooden ladder leading up to the trap door. For more discretion, they extinguished the torch before ascending and Carys went out first. She didn't trust the earl not to have posted guards to intercept them, despite his promise not to do so. When she saw no one, she called out to James that it was safe to come out.

Once out in the bailey she watched him take in deep gulps of fresh, flower-scented air. Her heart squeezed in compassion. How sweet it would taste to a man who'd spent a whole day and night in a dungeon, and thought he was about to die. She, too, felt as if she had been given her life back.

But they had to hurry. Dawn was not far. Over the horizon, they could already distinguish the pikes of the forest at the top of the hill.

"Go find Mistress Ivy," she told him urgently. "Tell her what happened. I'm sure she will help—"

"Don't worry about me. Now I'm out of that hell hole, I'll be just fine." James drew her into the shadow of the keep when the moon appeared from behind a cloud, illuminating them, and then took her into his arms. "Thank you, Carys. I have no idea how to repay you for what you did."

"One or two ideas come to mind." She had the satisfaction of hearing him growl in her ear. Apparently, he'd had the same ideas.

"And so I'm leaving. Again." He sighed, his forehead against hers. "Will you wait for me? Again?"

"Yes, I will wait for you. Again. And always."

Chapter Fifteen

Five days later, James was back.

It had been the longest five days in Carys' life. The king had lingered for longer than she had expected, testing everyone's temper with his boasts about his victories in battle and her patience by declaring his brave men should get a well-deserved rest while they were being offered such lavish hospitality. No one in the retinue caught the merest glimpse of Branwen during their stay, since she stayed in her rooms, as promised. Matthew had told his guests on the day of their arrival that his wife was not to tax herself at this time.

"I'm afraid you will have to contend with me alone," he said as soon as the refreshments had been served. His tone brooked no argument. "Branwen is heavy with child and having a hard time of it all."

"Of course," the king soothed with more understanding than Carys had expected. Perhaps, having had more than a dozen children with Queen Eleanor, his wife who'd died almost a decade ago, he knew all about the issues women with child faced. "By all means, let her get the rest she needs."

At least there had been a small consolation. The Earl of

Lancaster had left Sheridan Manor as soon as his uncle had arrived, offering the weakest of excuses. It seemed he wasn't sure his host would not come to stab him in the night to avenge his wife, and perhaps he was right to fear such an eventuality. The look Matthew had thrown him when they had met after the assault had chilled Carys to the marrow. It was clear he cared not about what arrangements had been made and would seize the first opportunity to make him pay for what he had done to Branwen. In the earl's place, she would have fled as well.

They were well rid of the foul man.

After four excruciatingly long days, the king took his leave. Once the retinue was gone, Matthew decided to wait for another day before calling James back, just to be on the safe side. Then he sent William, the little page to the village to get him.

And so at last, one Sunday evening, Carys watched him ride through the gate on his black stallion.

Rooted to the spot, she drank him in, taking in the freshly shaven jaw, the determination burning in his eyes, the beloved black tunic. He was back, he was safe, he was here.

She could start breathing again.

Matthew was at his side in an instant, clasping his arm in a manly handshake. "Dear God, James. I don't know what to say. I never got to thank you before you left. You saved my wife from that bastard Lancaster, and almost died because of your courage."

He ran a hand through his hair, his face a picture of anguish. Carys knew how hard it had been for him to know his beloved wife was being assaulted and not be able to do anything for her. He blamed himself for not having been at Sheridan Manor to welcome the earl in her stead, for having left at such a critical time. Branwen had assured him she did not blame him, that no real harm had been done but Carys could tell he'd only agreed to ease her mind. Deep down he still felt responsible. She could only hope that, in time, he would learn to shed the guilt.

"There is nothing, *nothing* I could do that will ever express my gratitude, but know that you have it nonetheless."

"Please, I don't need your gratitude, as long as I can have your affection." James landed a hand on the younger man's shoulder, the gesture paternal.

"You've always had it. I'm proud to count myself as the son you weren't able to see grow up."

There was a pause, charged with emotion. Then James cleared his throat. "I could not have asked for a better one."

Carys wiped a tear from her cheek as she watched the two men nod at one another, the gesture somehow more meaningful than if they had fallen into each other's arms. She of all people knew the link that could bind two strangers and, in that moment, they did look like father and son.

"Now, come. Branwen has asked to see you when you came back. She, too, would like to thank you for what you did."

"I'll be glad to go to her as soon as I'm able. But if you will excuse me, right now there is something I need to do, something I've been prevented from doing for far too long."

Matthew's face did not betray any surprise, but his brown eyes were gleaming when he turned to look at her. "Of course. You do that. I will give orders to ensure that you are not disturbed."

Carys felt herself blush to the roots of her hair. Not only had he guessed what that mysterious thing was, but he was giving his approval. There was no mistaking the warmth in his eyes. Would he go tell Branwen her adoptive mother and his second father had formed an attachment? Her daughter already suspected it, she was sure of it. Would she and her husband talk about what the future might bring?

Did it matter? No. Carys was not ashamed.

Let them think and say what they will, since she was certain they approved anyway.

Without further ado, James took her by the hand to lead her to his room. She didn't even think to protest, didn't utter a word, she simply allowed him to take her where he wanted—where they both wanted. Her heart started to beat a fierce rhythm when he closed the door behind him.

This was it. The moment they had waited so long for.

Instead of feeling shy, she felt thirty years younger.

"This could take a while. So I will be a bit cleverer than the other lovers at Sheridan Manor and ensure no one disturbs us, shall I?" He bolted the door as he spoke.

"Please."

She would die if anyone interrupted them now. They had waited too long for this first joining. Years since their spouses' deaths and months since they'd found one another. They had been thwarted at every turn, prevented to act on the desire they felt.

No more.

James stood in front of her, a tower of strength. Her core started to tingle in anticipation. Before she could say anything he lifted her into his arms, forcing her to wrap her arms around his neck and her legs around his waist, like he had that day in the sea.

"Carys, without you I would be dead, or married to Margaret. In more ways than one, I owe you my life," he told her, eyes aglow. "I think it's only fair you get to take charge of it from now on. Tell me how I can serve you?"

As if he couldn't guess. Under her buttocks she could feel the proof that they might want the same thing. "I think you know what I want right now. But first, you could kiss me."

Everything dissolved within her when he took her lips in a

fierce kiss. The salt from the sea wasn't there today, but there was spice, and all the sweetness she craved. It was even better.

"As much as I would like to take you here where we stand, I will take you to bed," he said, speaking with his mouth at her throat. "I'm no green lad anymore."

"And I am no lithe damsel. A bed will be just perfect." She smiled, before taking his earlobe between her lips. "But before anything else, I'll need to see you naked."

"You will. You will see every inch of me. It's all yours anyway."

He deposited her onto the bed gently, and proceeded to undress with unhurried gestures that built her anticipation to an almost unbearable level. When he was naked at the foot of the bed, she stared in disbelief. Had any man been more beautiful? Carys addressed a mental thanks to his mother for allowing the Egyptian merchant's charms to sway her, because the result was pure perfection. No one she had ever met had such mouth-watering, sun-kissed skin.

"I've imagined this moment countless times, you know." Kneeling on the bed, she placed a hand over his chest. To her delight, it was as firm and hairy as she had imagined it. So virile... "You're just like you appeared in my dreams." He *was* dark all over, and his manhood as deliciously tempting as she had hoped.

"You've dreamed of me?" He sounded both surprised and pleased at the notion.

"Yes." Admitting such a forbidden thing felt wicked but she couldn't lie.

"Were you naked in that dream?"

"Yes."

"Was I?"

"Yes."

"Mm." Sleek and determined, he leaned in toward her,

forcing her to lie back down on the soft mattress. Once she was flat on her back, he loomed over her, his weight supported by two muscular arms. "Tell me, what did I do to you in those dreams, you maddening woman? Or perhaps I don't need to ask if we were both naked... Still, I'd like to hear it."

"You spoke to me in Welsh, for a start."

His eyebrows shot upwards. "That is *not* what I had thought you'd say, and not something I will be able to do today, I'm afraid. But whatever else I did in that dream of yours to bring you pleasure, I can do in real life. I'm not the shy kind."

Heat bolted through her veins. She knew he wasn't a shy sort of lover, rather the scandalous sort. And with him, so was she. "You came to my bed and started to caress me. It was wonderful but I woke up before I could reach my peak. It was rather frustrating."

"I bet it was." His voice became impossibly husky and his nose lowered until it was touching her temple. "Tell me what you did to ease that frustration."

Carys moaned. How had the wretched man guessed she had not left it at that? And now he was asking her to describe what she had done. It had not been a question, but an order. Just like that day at the beach, he was forcing her to be crude. And he was waiting for her to start... It was clear he would not move until she had told him what she had done to herself in excruciating detail.

"Could I do it in Welsh?"

A slow smile was all the answer she got. An agreement of sorts, one she seized gratefully. Cheeks aflame, she started to describe how she had run her fingers along her folds before dipping into her soaked flesh and bringing herself to an explosive release.

By the time she was done, her need for his touch had been

brought to a fever pitch and James' eyes were two glittering obsidians.

"Bloody hell," he growled, his mouth still in her hair. "I really need to start learning Welsh. I would give a fortune to understand what you just said."

Well, she would be only too glad to teach him but the lessons would have to wait. For now she had to ease the burning inside her body.

Carys started to shed her clothes with more impatience than grace. Now that they were assured they would not be interrupted, James behaved as if they had all the time in the world, forcing her to talk, teasing her, looming over her without ever touching her. Perhaps they did have all the time in the world, but she was desperate to start. Her dress was sent flying across the room, and her shift soon followed.

"Bloody hell," he repeated, once she had bared her body. It had been years since anyone had seen her naked. Any doubt Carys might have about her body vanished the moment James growled his approval.

She lay back down and he followed, caging her under him once more.

None too gently, as if he'd been driven to the edge of his control by the sight of her, he cupped her right breast and latched onto her nipple with the eagerness of a starved man. She remembered thinking how much she missed a man's mouth on her when she had given herself pleasure that day after her dream. There it was, as hot and satisfying as it could be. Groaning in time with her moans, he suckled her so thoroughly that he rendered her breathless with need. She forgot her intention to disrobe completely. Delicious as this was, she couldn't wait another moment to feel him surge within her. She would remove her stockings and shoes later.

"James, please take me," she rasped, her voice barely recognizable. "I can't stand any more teasing."

They'd had months of it. She needed him *now*.

"No, neither can I." He sounded on the verge of desperation himself. "I wanted to pleasure you first, but I will just have to do that afterward. Either way, unlike in your dream, I promise you will be satisfied."

Carys had a suspicion they would be too drained afterward to do anything other than lie in each other's arms but she nodded nonetheless. No need to ensure her satisfaction beforehand, she already knew his possession would be enough to make her explode in release.

A heartbeat later, she was proven right. His first thrust had to be the most extraordinary thing she had ever felt, slow, hot, hard, and everything in between. Her body started to tighten, heat bolted to the base of her skull. No! Too soon!

"Wait!" she cried out, desperate to savor this first joining to the full. She wanted to stay balanced on the edge of release a little while longer, make the most of the moment. "It's... too good."

"Yes. Too good."

James stilled and, to her delight, closed his mouth over her nipple again, licking it, teasing it, sucking it as deep as it would go into his mouth. She started to circle her hips and it was too much. There was no stopping the sensations unfurling through her body.

She was blooming, just like that plant reviving under gentle rain she had once likened herself to.

Her core started to spasm in time with the suckling, her muscles clamped over the length buried inside her, starting a pulsing that seemed to come from the very depth of her soul. It was unlike anything she had ever experienced, quiet, intimate, and oh so delicious. She had not suspected she could ever reached her peak without feeling her lover move but here she was, being ripped apart by pleasure.

"Yessss." The word was one, long moan of ecstasy. What was he doing to her?

"Christ, Carys, you feel so good. I want more," James whispered against her breast. "I want all of you. Now."

"Take what you need. Now."

She wanted to feel him move. She wanted to soar again.

And then she wanted *him* to do the same.

He withdrew, then slowly, inch by inch, he filled her again. Dear God, it had been too long since she had felt a man surge inside her, too long since she had wanted *this* man to fill her, for her not to be overwhelmed. The tryst by the beach, scandalous, satisfying as it had been, had not been the same. Nothing compared to feeling your body tighten around your lover's member, to having his heat inside you.

This possession was nothing like her husband's had been, less hurried, more intimate, less familiar, more forbidden, all new and wonderful. Overwhelming. James seemed to think the same thing. Poised above her, he was trembling.

"Are you all right?" She closed her arms around him protectively. He had stopped moving and she thought she knew what the issue might be.

"I have not... Not since..."

Her heart bled for him, because she understood what he was unable to say. He meant he'd not been able to let himself go, to experience his pleasure to the full since his sons' deaths, too worried about the consequences of getting a woman with child.

"I know, but you can with me, remember? You can let go. I'll be with you all the way." She stroked his back, still strong and smooth, if perhaps not as firm as it would have been years ago. "It is as if we had been made for one another. With me, what you fear won't happen. We can share our lives, our woes, our hopes, our pleasure together."

"Aye."

Surrounded by Carys' words and comforting warmth, James could feel his doubts melt away, his body heat up, his life become brighter. He gave a tentative thrust, then another, more forceful. She moaned and arched her back. He'd already felt her spasm around him in a languorous, slow release but she needed more. As did he. He could feel the tension building in his veins, the effort it took him not to surrender to his need to pound into her. Because as soon as he increased the rhythm, he would erupt.

Could he let go? Yes, perhaps with her, he could.

"Carys." Her name was little more than a plea.

"Yes, it's me. I'm here with you. Don't be afraid of your pleasure. Let it come." Her hands at his buttocks, she held him tight, keeping him sheathed deep inside her warmth. "Please, James, I need more, I need you."

The plea broke through the last of his resistance. This was not about him, but about Carys and what she deserved to have. She was not a virgin, she was not new to pleasure, she wanted this, she deserved the best he could give her. If she needed him, she would have him.

Draping one of her legs around his waist to allow for deeper penetration, he started to pump his hips. All the while he looked deep into her eyes, increasing the connection between them. With anyone else such raw intimacy would have felt uncomfortable. With the woman who had saved him from a miserable fate and even death, it just felt right. He was about to give her what he'd never thought to give anyone else in his life.

She smiled at him—and it started. A boiling at the base of his spine. A need for release. There would be no stopping it now, and for the first time in two decades, he didn't want to stop it. All the air left his lungs. He reared up.

"Holy fuck, I'm..."

The rest of the sentence was covered by Carys' own cry of release. To feel him trusting her, allowing himself to possess her without worrying about the possible consequences had sent her over the edge. The speed with which she reached her second peak told him it had been too long since she had felt her body erupt around her lover. And the moment was too beautiful for him not to follow her into the abyss.

"Stay with me," she rasped, feeling the force of his thrusts increase. Inside her, she meant, until the end.

"Yes." The word was little more than a gasp.

He collapsed, felled by a release so powerful he had no choice but to surrender to it. At the last moment he rolled off her, careful not to crush her under his weight.

James waited for the inevitable moment of panic. It never came. Instead, peace invaded him. He'd made it. Never again would he be afraid, because the woman in his arms was the only woman he would bed from now on.

He took her hand in his, and kissed the palm softly, gratitude and love swelling in his chest.

"I *will* stay with you, Carys. Always."

The banging on the door was so loud it woke Carys up with a start. In front of her was a window she didn't recognize and it took her a moment to understand where she was. Then she felt the weight of a masculine hand on her naked breast and everything came back to her in one luminous rush.

James.

Their night together. His body over her, his heat around

her, his strength inside her. The tender words, the pleasure, the trust, the wonderful release, the falling asleep in each other's arms. A smile stretched her lips. Their first lovemaking had been a rebirth, for both of them. And the second one, in the middle of the night, had been just as perfect, if somewhat more frenzied.

Now that they had shared a night together, they would get the second chance at life they craved.

Still half asleep, warm and loath to shake off the delicious torpor bathing her body, she covered his hand with hers and squeezed. James groaned and tightened his hold around her breast.

"Mm, yes, mine," he said, his voice little more than a growl. Her breath hitched when he started to play with her hardening nipple, pinching it lightly. Was he about to—

The banging started again, more insistent. James' eyes snapped open and he glared at the door as if he had the power to skewer whoever was on the other side with his stare.

"What is it?" The sensual growl he'd used with her had become a bark.

"Forgive me. Branwen is asking after her mother," Richard's voice called out. "Her pains have started."

Carys bolted upright, fully awake. Branwen was in labor? Already? They weren't expecting her to give birth for another month at the very least. What was going on? Either Mistress Ivy had gotten the date of conception wrong or the babe was early. Lord almighty, please let it not be a problem. Would she know no peace? Just when she'd been thinking her life was perfect, this had to happen!

Everything within her surged. Dear God, her daughter needed her and here she was, lounging in bed after a night of debauchery. Then she realized what she'd heard. Richard had been sent to get her and he'd come to James' room? How had he guessed she would be here? Did he know what had happened between her and his friend or had Matthew told him that was where she would be? He'd seemed to guess what James needed to do the day before. Matthew, Branwen, Richard. Did anyone else at Sheridan Manor know about them?

There was no time to worry about it now. She had to get to her daughter, who was waiting for her.

"Well, don't just lie there, you big oaf, help me get dressed!" she cried, jumping out of the bed. Her clothes were scattered about the room, a reminder of the previous night's activities, and it would take more time than she wanted to get ready, time she did not have.

Branwen needed her.

James groaned and grumbled as he did so, but he did get up to help her. "Oaf... If it's all the same to you, I'd rather you stuck to Welsh when you insult me, that way I might not feel the sting of it so much."

Carys instantly regretted the outburst. It was not his fault she was fretting, and he had done nothing wrong. She turned to him, an apology already on her lips—and stilled at the sight of his naked body. Lord, had she ever seen a more arousing sight? Nothing less than the birth of her first grandchild could have dragged her away from him in this moment. The look he gave her told her he was thinking the same thing. At any other time he would have dragged her back into bed and let her kiss every inch of him.

Ignoring the temptation he presented, she lifted her shift above her head and let it fall down in one swoop. The dress proved more of a challenge, however. She gave a series of curses under her breath, in Welsh this time, as she fumbled with it. Why did she have to wear, today of all days, the only gown she possessed which laced at the back?

James, who'd retrieved her second shoe from under the bed, placed a hand over her shoulder.

"Let me." She nodded in gratitude. He'd seen her struggle and understood she was on the verge of panic. He wanted to help. She almost started to sob. With quick, efficient moves, he put her to rights, then placed a swift kiss in the crook of her neck. "All done."

"Thank you." Not bothering with the stockings she hadn't been able to locate, she started to fasten her shoes. "Now I need to go."

"Wait. Carys." Before she could reach the door, he drew her into his arms, facing him, and looked deep into her eyes. He was still naked, and deliciously warm against her. "I love you. I know the moment is ill-chosen to say it, but I do. I could not let you leave my bed without you knowing it because I do not want you to worry that this night we shared means nothing to me. It was not just a night, it was the start of something beautiful, as beautiful as you are." He gave a rueful smile and brought his mouth to her ear. "I had intended to take you again this morning and tell you I loved you while I was inside you but I hadn't counted on Matthew's son wanting to be born today."

Carys melted. Had anyone ever heard a more moving declaration? Perhaps, but *she* had not.

"There is never a bad time to tell someone you love them, I don't think." Although she would have liked to be told while he was deep inside her, this was just as good. As long as she heard the words, she cared not when or how it happened. And he was right. This was the start of something new and they were done with waiting. Every moment had to be seized. "So I will tell you before going that I love you too."

Only the twinkle in his eyes betrayed his amusement when he said, his face as impassive as usual, "I thought you might. You certainly behaved as if you did last night. Or perhaps you only wanted the pleasure my body could give you."

The teasing earned him a tap on the chest. "Awful man! As to Matthew, I fear you've been listening to him too much. This child might be a daughter."

James shook his head. "He knows. Just like somehow, both times, I knew with my sons that they would be boys. I trust him. If he says it's a son, then that's what it is."

Carys nodded slowly. She had heard Branwen say many times that she was convinced she was carrying a boy, without being able to explain why. So perhaps there was something in this new parent's instinct. Unfortunately, she would never know.

"Either way, this child will be loved," she said, placing a kiss next to his nipple, where the skin was warm and soft. "He has a big family waiting for him."

"Yes." James sounded suspiciously hoarse. Was he moved or aroused? Both? Before she could wonder further, he cleared his throat and gave her a tap on the buttocks. "Now, go and deliver our first grandchild."

Chapter Sixteen

T he moans never quite became screams, and they were all the more heart-wrenching for it, because they betrayed Branwen's exhaustion, anguish and determination to save her strength to help her baby along when the moment came. Carys had no idea what to do, save murmur soothing words in Welsh and bathe her forehead with a cool cloth.

The powerlessness was killing her but at least she was reassured on one point. Mistress Ivy had assured them that, although the babe was on the early side, there was nothing to worry about.

"I've delivered plenty such babies in my time. They just come when they're ready, there is no stopping them. Born in the warm months, and with proper care, he will not suffer," the woman had concluded in her soothing, matter-of-fact way.

She'd also warned them that first babies could take rather a long time to come into the world. Unfortunately, that prediction had proven all too true. Branwen had been laboring all day and for the best part of the night now, and it was showing. Her face was drawn, her hair matted with sweat, her movements slower, testimony to the strain put on her body. Would she have enough strength left to deliver the child? Having no experience of giving birth herself to calm her nerves, Carys felt utterly helpless, rather like a father-to-be would feel.

How ironic for a woman.

"Ah. Here we go," Mistress Ivy declared at long last, sounding impossibly cheerful. You could have sworn she had just arrived in the room. "Now you're going to have to push, my lady."

"Push!" Branwen made a sound that might have been a laugh in other circumstances. "What do you think I've been doing all this time?"

"This will feel different, you'll see."

"How will it—" Carys squeezed her daughter's hand in support because it was clear from the panic flaring in her eyes that she'd just understood what the woman was referring to. "Oh," she moaned. "No. I don't think I can't do this."

"Yes, you can. There is no other way."

This time Branwen did scream.

Just as the first ray of sun shot above the pink horizon, the baby slithered out of her exhausted body. Something happened in Carys' heart. It swelled, or tripped, or exploded, she wasn't sure quite which. Mayhap all three at once. This had been the most intense experience of her life.

"A beautiful son." She beamed as she watched the midwife clean the little body with competent gestures. The parents' instinct had been proven right, they had been gifted with a little boy. Not that they would have minded a daughter, she was sure.

"A son," Branwen repeated, sounding bewildered by the sudden ending to her torment. "I don't know why, but I just knew it would be a boy. Is everything all right? I can't hear him scream. Is he—"

"Everything is perfect, don't worry. Not all babies cry, you know," Mistress Ivy soothed, placing the babe in his mother's arms. Then she winked at Carys, as if the two of them shared a secret. "But some mothers, and even grandmothers, have been known to shed tears."

As if on cue, Branwen started sobbing and the single tear that had been gathering in Carys' eyes finally fell. For a long, beautiful moment mother and daughter hugged each other, the little boy nestled between them.

"I'm so proud of you, Branwen *bach*. Look at what you did. He's perfect."

"I know. I can't believe it. It's over and I have a beautiful babe as a reward for my efforts." Huge amber eyes lifted to her. "I want Matthew. Please, Mam, go get him, he will be beside himself with worry."

Without having seen the poor man, Carys knew her daughter was right. The midwife had been adamant that men were not allowed in the bedchamber during the birth. Branwen had been too racked with pain to argue and Matthew too intent on not getting on the bad side of the woman in charge of his wife's well-being to insist but Carys could not help but feel it had been a mistake to send him away. The parents-to-be would have borne the ordeal more easily if they had been together.

She gave her instructions to the maid stationed outside the door for that very purpose. "Go tell his lordship he can come now. The babe is born, and well. Then go to bed. You look about to collapse."

The girl nodded and disappeared down the spiral staircase.

Carys took the baby in her arms while Mistress Ivy dealt with the afterbirth and made Branwen more comfortable. Her whole body felt warm with joy. The little boy was perfect, so small yet already a person in his own right, with deep blue eyes and an impossibly small mouth. She could have watched him all day.

A moment later the door opened on a haggard Matthew. That he had not slept a wink that night was obvious. Pale, disheveled and unshaven, she had never seen him in such a state. He blanched when he saw that his wife was crying.

"Raven. Oh God, I'm so sorry, this is all my fault... I should never have— Are you all right?"

Branwen let out a laugh, the sound bursting through the last of her tears. "Yes, it is all your fault," she said, wiping at her cheeks with slightly shaky hands. "I would never have allowed anyone else to do it. You gave me the most wonderful little boy and I love you for it. Take your son and come to me. Please, I need you both."

Matthew walked up to Carys, looking guilty, as if he were loath to take the babe from her. But no one had more right to the little boy than he did. This man had given her daughter everything, his love, his protection, the life she deserved, a child to cherish. As if that was not enough, he had been the reason she and James had met. Had he not brought his new wife and her family to Sheridan Manor, she wouldn't now be in a position to enjoy the gift of a grandson and a life with a man she loved and who loved her.

Smiling, she handed him the bundled up baby. He took him with the ease of a man who loved children and knew how to take care of them. Branwen had told her many times how good he was with his nieces. Carys could see that it was no boast. Her son-in-law would be the father every child dreamed of, loving and attentive.

"He has Branwen's black hair," he whispered, as awed as if that were a miracle, or even unusal for a baby to look like his parents.

"He does. And he has your mouth, I think. A perfect little boy."

"Yes, perfect." The smile he gave her shot straight to her

heart. After one last nod in her direction, he walked over to the bed and bent to give his wife a tender kiss. "Oh, *cariad*, I thank you for this gift from the bottom of my heart. I'm so blessed to have you both."

Carys and Mistress Ivy exchanged a discreet glance. It was time for them to go. The new parents needed to be alone with their son.

"Now that my work is done, I think I will make use of the bed you asked to be prepared for me earlier," the healer told her once they had reached the floor below.

"Yes." Carys opened the door to her friend. "You deserve it. Thank you for what you did for my daughter."

"You're welcome. It was as I predicted, an easy, if somewhat lengthy birth. And with a husband like Matthew Hunter in her bed, your daughter will be blessed with many more children in the years to come."

"Let's hope so."

At the bottom of the staircase Carys took a moment to steady herself. Tears were threatening again. They seemed to want to come out of their own accord, which was hardly surprising after the emotional upheaval she had just been through. Then, all of a sudden, a hand landed on the small of her back, warm and comforting. No need to check who it was. She would have recognized James' touch everywhere and, anyway, who else would be so presumptuous? To her relief, Richard was now happy with Avice, who was a much better match for him than she would ever have been.

"Come, my love, don't stay here all alone," he purred. "You can cry all you like, but in my arms."

She turned around, buried her face against his chest and did just that. Nevertheless, as they were tears of joy, they did not last long. She drew away, feeling suddenly exhausted by the sleepless night and the outpouring of emotions. James was looking at her through slightly blurry eyes, his clothes were in disarray and his jaw was dark with stubble. He had never looked dearer to her.

"Have you slept at all?" she asked, even though she could guess the answer.

He gave an amused snort, confirming her suspicions. "And leave the lad alone in the great hall? I think not. Someone had to be there to keep him from tearing his hair out or drinking himself to death. I'm sorry to say that Richard wasn't much help, though this was not his first time becoming a grandfather. He was a wreck at the thought of having another grandson, and even Avice's food went untouched." He nodded toward the room at the top of the stairs where Matthew and Branwen were getting to know their son. "I have nothing against Mistress Ivy but the next time those two have a child, we will have to choose a midwife who lets him in with Branwen, because I'm not doing that again, not for all the gold in the world. Forget him, *my* nerves will not survive it."

Carys laughed through her lingering tears. "Yes. We will definitely have to do that, because I'm not having Branwen fretting again the way she did. I swear she was more worried about how Matthew was faring than her own discomfort. It didn't help to calm her down, as you can imagine."

"But all is well?" There was a note of worry in his voice. Of course he would have worried himself sick last night, without even being allowed to show it. He would have wanted to be strong for Matthew, and not let his fears show, but the events of the night would have brought back painful memories for him. Joanne had lost the daughter who had come early and their second child, though it had been born at the right time, had not survived the birth. "That was an awfully long labor."

"All is well. Mistress Ivy had warned us first babies often take longer to be born and she was certainly proven right. But

Branwen was magnificent." Tears threatened again but Carys ruthlessly pushed them away. "She was so brave, I'm so proud of her."

"She's your true daughter then." There was such love and emotion in his voice that she gave another sob. What was the man doing, speaking to her thus when she was already an emotional mess? If he carried on like this, she might not be able to refrain from crying "Come, let's get you something to drink, and one of Avice's famous honey tarts."

"Yes. " That sounded heavenly. She hadn't realized she was famished as well as parched, but it was little wonder if she was. She had barely had time to snatch a sip or two of ale during Branwen's labor. Trust James to think of everything.

"While he carved a groove in the stone floor with his pacing, Matthew told me the name they intended to give their son," James informed her while he poured them both a cup of ale.

"Oh?" Lost to the relief of seeing baby and mother were well, Carys had forgotten to ask about the name. She looked at him expectantly but he didn't offer any more explanation. "Well, are you going to tell me what it is?" she said, accepting the ale.

He made a grimace. "That's the thing. I can't. It's a Welsh name I cannot for the life of me repeat. Something like Yorwar."

A smile tugged at her lips at the way he butchered the name. She would have to teach him her language, as she was sure to enjoy hearing his take on familiar words. "I think you mean Iorwerth."

"Perhaps."

He looked so put out that, unable to resist, she kissed him full on the lips, heedless of who might see them. In any case, the people at Sheridan Manor had better get used to the notion that the steward was no longer a free man.

He was now *her* man, and soon, everyone would know it.

"Worry not, my love. I'll teach you how to pronounce it properly. Or you could find a nickname for him, something to be used just for you. He's your grandson, you can do what you like."

His eyes lit up in relief, the dark in them shining like obsidian. So beautiful. "I could, couldn't I?"

The joy on his face was too much. Carys knew how much this birth would mean to him, who had lost all four of his children and, with them, all hope of ever having grandchildren. It meant as much as it meant to her.

They each had been given a second chance at family, thanks to the two people they had adopted as children of their hearts, and it was just perfect that way.

"Have you eaten enough?" James asked once she had enjoyed two of the tarts. The spring sun was illuminating the hall, turning everything golden around them.

"Yes."

Without further ado, he swept her into his arms. "Then, it's off to bed with you. You need a good sleep, as do I. And then when we wake up, I'll do what I intended to do yesterday morning. Twice."

Epilogue

Dusk was descending over the land, throwing broad stripes of pink, crimson and gold over the flawless blue sky. James had come to the battlements to watch the sun set over a glorious day. He smiled. All the days had been glorious of late, or so it seemed.

Next to him, Carys let out a happy sigh, echoing his feelings. "I could stay and watch them forever," she murmured in his ear.

"I know. Me too."

Down below was a scene of domestic bliss he would never tire of. Branwen was singing a Welsh ballad to little Yoyo while Matthew cradled their newborn daughter as if she were the most precious thing in the world. In a way, she was, of course. The babe had been born just over a week ago, this time with her father in attendance, and she had already won everyone's heart, including that of her eighteen-month-old brother.

To add to James' delight, the name that had been chosen for her, Rhian, was relatively easy to pronounce. No matter how much he was trying, he just could not match Matthew's ease with the fiendish Welsh language. A lesser man would have surrendered by now and he was sorely tempted to give up. He only persisted because the spark igniting in his wife's eyes when he tried to say anything never failed to warm his insides.

In the months since their wedding, he had grown to love her more than he thought possible.

"Carys. Your parents called you 'beloved' when you were born. Then Dewi made sure the name could apply to you all through the first part of your life. Now, if you will allow me, it will be my honor and privilege to ensure you feel it is the most fitting name you could have been given for the rest of our lives together," he'd told her as they'd exchanged their vows in the little chapel at Sheridan Manor.

Eyes filled with tears, his bride had only been able to nod.

"Do you know what is odd about seeing Branwen married and with children of her own?" she said, talking to herself as was her wont. "In my mind, I am still her age. In my mind, I am young enough to be Iorwerth and Rhian's mother."

"I know exactly what you mean, and let me assure you that you look nothing like a wizened grandmother." James whispered, his mouth at her temple. Her delighted giggle warmed him all the way to his toes.

"And you look nothing like a wrinkled old man."

"That may be because I am married to a woman who brings the best out in me. It keeps me young at heart, and in my mind, I look just like him." He nodded toward Matthew who was nuzzling at his daughter's neck. "Only with darker hair."

"Yes. Darker everything, for my delight." Carys let out another sigh, wistful this time. "They have a family, and their whole lives ahead of them. It's hard not to be envious."

Just then, the babe let out a wail. Matthew instantly started to pace in a soothing rhythm up and down the rose-bordered alley. He had done little else than rock his daughter to sleep in the past week, or so it seemed. James felt another smile tug at his lips and he leaned in to speak into Carys' ear.

"Yes, they are young and in love. But so are we. In love, I mean." He gave her a long, lingering kiss to prove the truth of his words. He felt better than he had in years. "And they have a crying babe to look after. Whereas we... *we* have nothing to stop ourselves from spending the night in exactly the way we want."

With a flourish, he lifted her into his arms. Carys let out a gasp, as he'd hoped she would. He knew she loved it when he acted extravagantly. As her husband, he had learned to be more spontaneous. It was impossible to remain stern when in the company of someone like his little Welsh miracle. He now owned no fewer than three colored tunics, even if he still favored black, and he had been known on occasion to laugh out loud at Yoyo's antics.

It was liberating, the life he had thought lost forever.

"Am I to understand you have plans for the night, Master Mortimer? Plans that involve me?" Carys asked, her voice hoarse with longing.

He let out a purr. All his plans involved her, in some way or another, and they would continue to do so until the rest of his life. He could not wait.

"Take me to bed, Mistress Mortimer, and you will see."

A Rogue for Siân
Read about Christopher and Siân

About the Author

As far back as I remember, I have been attracted to the Middle Ages, to knights in shining armour and their ladies in spectacular dresses. Now I get to write about them, I feel like the luckiest woman in the world. Being French and married to a Brit makes each book I write extra special, as our countries share a long and sometimes painful past. But in the end, in life as well as in fiction, love conquers all!

I have published several medieval romances under my own name, including series, and also have a pen name, Judith Falcon, for spicier projects, still in historical romance.

Join my newsletter and check out my other books on virginiemarconato.com.

Also by Virginie Marconato

The Welsh Rebels

A Husband for Esyllt

A Savior for Branwen

A Second Chance for Carys

A Rogue for Siân

The Noble Norsemen

Taming the Wolf

Soothing the Beast

Wooing the Devil

Baiting the Bear

Tempting the Saxon

Seducing the Warrior

Loving the Blacksmith